# MARTIN RIDES THE MOOR

It was snowing heavily. Martin snuggled down in bed. He felt sorry for anyone out on a night like this. That was the first time he remembered the pony in the orchard. He tried to sleep, but he couldn't forget the pony. He kept seeing pictures. He saw the snow crusting the pony's head and back, making its mane as wet as rain. He kept seeing its dejection because nobody cared.

But he did care. This little pony needed him because it had nobody else. Then he felt the wind. He knew what the wind would do. It would carry the snow in white clouds, making deep drifts. That was what covered sheep and cattle. That was what buried ponies.

Martin moved. He was out of bed so suddenly that the cold didn't matter. He had to go out to the orchard and bring the pony in.

3cde

Also by Vian Smith

PARADE OF HORSES
COME DOWN THE MOUNTAIN

and published by CAROUSEL BOOKS

Vian Smith

# Martin Rides
# the Moor

Illustrated by PETER FORSTER

Carousel Editor: Anne Wood

**CAROUSEL BOOKS**
A DIVISION OF TRANSWORLD PUBLISHERS LTD

# MARTIN RIDES THE MOOR

A CAROUSEL BOOK 0 552 52041 1

Originally published in Great Britain
by Constable Young Books Ltd.

PRINTING HISTORY
Constable Young edition published 1964
Carousel edition published 1974

Copyright © 1964 by Vian Smith

This book is set in 12-on-13pt Baskerville

Carousel Books are published by Transworld
Publishers Ltd.,
Cavendish House, 57–59 Uxbridge Road,
Ealing, London, W.5

Made and printed in Great Britain by
Cox & Wyman Ltd., London, Reading and Fakenham

**N.B. The Australian price appearing on the
back cover is the recommended retail price.**

*To*
*TUPPENCE*
*THE MOORLAND PONY OF*
*THIS STORY*

# CHAPTER ONE

THE pony came to the edge of the ramp. Its head was up, its ears were sharp. It looked around to the orchard, the shippens, the farmhouse. It stared a long time at the moor which rose above the farm.

Harvey stood on one side of the lorry, Jane on the other. He was the pony-farmer from whom the pony had been bought. She was his ten-year-old daughter. They had brought it to the Manninghams of Shepherds Hill. Now they watched to see what would happen.

Nathan, the farm-hand, nudged the halter. For a moment the pony resisted. Then it put one foot on the straw which covered the ramp. One foot meant two feet. Nathan kept it going until suddenly the pony was out of the lorry and in the orchard lane. It turned quickly, trying to see everything at once. Nathan patted its neck. Then he looked to Martin, waiting for the boy to show a sign.

Martin was eleven years old. He guessed that this was supposed to be a big occasion, that his father had planned it carefully, hoping to surprise him. Martin knew that many boys of his age would be delighted and grateful. But the delight was not there. Neither was the gratitude.

He could not forget that he was different now.

Different from other boys who had been his friends at school; different from Jane who was his only friend on the moor. He could not forget that he had been made different by this silence which had come suddenly, bewildering him and so frightening his parents that they didn't know what to do.

The pony was the idea of parents who didn't know what to do. It was a gift. He was supposed to go hunting, to compete in gymkhanas. He was supposed to pretend that nothing had happened, that he could take his place among other boys and girls. Martin thought his parents didn't understand. He didn't want to ride, to hunt, to pretend that nothing had happened. He didn't want to try because he didn't believe it. He knew how different he had become. Now he felt his parents watching. His mother was smiling, hiding her anxiety, begging him to be what they wanted him to be. His father's eyes were begging, too. But behind the begging was a tightening impatience.

Martin didn't glance to Jane. He didn't glance to Harvey, who was boasting about the pony. He glanced to Nathan, hoping the grizzled old farm-hand would understand.

Nathan held the halter, stroking the pony's face. The pony was a Dartmoor. It had been foaled on the moor and Harvey had brought it in and chosen it for breaking. Jane had helped in the breaking. She'd been helping her father since she was six.

Now Mr. Manningham had bought it, trying to please his son. Martin knew what they wanted him to say.

'Thank you, it's lovely.'

The words were in his head, but when he tried to speak the words wouldn't come. It had often been like this. He was afraid of speaking, of feeling the effort in his throat, then of hearing nothing. Not to hear your own voice when you speak. That was something he hadn't grown used to yet. He looked at his mother. Her smile encouraged him to risk it. Finally he said, 'Thank you, it's very nice.' Then he shot Jane a glance, defying her to laugh because his voice was wrong.

Once he had seen a play, and in the play there had been a comic character, very funny. This comic character had cupped a hand behind his ear and said, 'Eh?', showing that he was deaf. The audience had roared, making deafness a very funny thing.

He had not cared then. That had been before the accident, and deafness had not mattered. It had been only something that happened to others, usually to the old. But now it was different. Now it mattered. Now it had happened to him.

His father came near. Martin did not hear the footsteps, but he felt his father coming. There was a tremor of fear, not because he was afraid of his father but because he was ashamed and resentful. He guessed that deafness made him seem a fool.

He thought his father would speak, speaking loudly the way people do to the deaf. He could always tell when his father was shouting. The impatience in the eyes gave it away. But this time his father did not shout. Mr. Manningham held out a hand, showing Martin the hand so he would not be shocked by a sudden touch. The hand asked to be trusted and Martin went with him towards the pony.

Now Nathan was smiling. So were Harvey and Jane. They were trying to bring him and the pony together. They tried too hard too soon. To Martin the pony was not something marvellous. It was just a Dartmoor, a mongrel like all the ponies which roamed the moor. It had a shaggy mane and ragged tail.

The pony flinched from his touch and the flinching showed that it wanted him no more than he wanted it. He could hear nothing, but its flared nostrils showed that it was snorting.

Nathan held the halter tightly with one hand. With the other he groped in a pocket and brought out a carrot. He snapped it, putting one end between his teeth and jerking downwards. He gave the pieces to Martin and Martin put them on his flattened palm, offering them to the pony. It backed, it threw its head. Nathan said, 'Been knocked about, don't trust nobody.'

But Martin did not hear. He supposed the pony was suspicious of him because he was different. Perhaps the pony sensed something different. He knew that in some ways animals were more sensitive than humans.

'So nervous,' Mrs. Manningham said. 'Would it be safe for Martin to ride?'

Nathan looked down. He doubted it. A deaf boy needed a safe pony. One that would plod across the moor, never startled by sudden sounds, never interested in the short way home. Nathan thought Mr. Manningham had made a bad buy and would regret it. Mr. Manningham had begun to think so, too. But Harvey tried to convince them. He was afraid the deal would fall through.

He said, 'The pony's young, fast, just what a boy needs.'

Mrs. Manningham wasn't convinced. She looked at the pony with deepening mistrust.

'Anyway,' her husband said, 'it's on trial for a fortnight.'

Martin knew they were talking and suspected they were talking about him. He was tired of people talking about him. He turned away, bored with the pony. He was cold and wanted to go in.

Mr. Manningham said to Nathan, 'Turn it out. Up the orchard.' To Harvey he added, 'We can see what happens in a day or two. If the pony's no good, the deal's off.'

Harvey muttered agreement, darting the boy a glance of disgust. Jane followed her father to the cab of the horse-box. They drove away, down the steep road to the bridge. Their farm was three miles away.

Martin watched Nathan lead the pony towards the orchard. Its step was lively, its head was bold. He turned towards the porch. He wasn't interested. He looked to the sky, feeling the threat of snow.

The table was ready for tea. Martin sat with his mother on the side nearer the glass cupboard and the old photograph of grandparents. His father sat on the other, his back to the clock, to the framed photographs of ploughing teams in the days of horses.

Martin glanced from one parent to the other.

They weren't talking. They were disappointed, with his father much more disappointed than his mother. He sensed that in a way his mother was relieved. She had always wanted to fuss him, because he was their only child. Since the accident she had fussed him more and more. He guessed that this fussing irritated his father. Mr. Manningham wanted him to be like other boys, to fight back, to prove that the accident hadn't changed him completely. Well, it had, and whose fault was that? Martin stole a glare, remembering how his father had encouraged him to swim, taking no notice when he'd said he didn't like it. 'Come on,' his father had said, 'be a man. You don't want to be a cissy, the only one who can't swim.' So he had tried to swim, and now they knew. The doctors said that swimming might have caused his deafness.

Martin sent another glare across the table. This time his father felt it and looked up. For a long moment their eyes met. He saw his father redden, then look down. He wanted to say, 'Your fault. A pony can't make up for that.'

Suddenly his father was talking angrily to the mother. Martin guessed what he was saying. The anger, the gestures, the glances told him. What else can a man do? That's what his father was saying. You give him a pony, a young, fast pony, most boys of his age would give anything for a pony. You try to make it a surprise, hoping he'll be grateful, laughing and excited like he used to be. And what happens? He turns away, he couldn't care less.

Then Martin glanced to his mother. She was answering, comforting the father, begging him to be patient. It's been a terrible shock. You can't expect him to be like other boys. That's what his mother was saying.

Martin made a moaning sound. He was tired of seeing them arguing, one impatient, the other begging for time. He thought he made the sound in his head. But their glances told him he had made it aloud. They seemed surprised, as though when you're deaf you can understand nothing. Then both were ashamed.

His mother got up to put more logs on the fire. She turned, hugging herself, showing him how cold it was.

'Cold enough for snow.'

Her mouth shaped the words carefully. Then she acted with gestures to explain the words. It was her way of making sure he understood. Martin knew what snow could mean. He glanced to his father. Mr. Manningham was watching the window, hoping his wife was wrong but knowing she was right.

# CHAPTER TWO

SNOW fell in the early darkness. It came down gently, pretending to be pretty, like a Christmas card. Within a hour it formed a white crust, making the old moor new. In another hour the crust was deep. By nine o'clock the moor was as silent as a graveyard.

Martin saw it from the landing window as he went to bed.

His first instinct was excitement, remembering how last year he had tobogganed with Jane. They had come hurtling down the hill, their shouts loud on the still air. He listened a long time to the shouting. It was in his memory. Then he saw the lantern. Its yellow light flooded the snow. The lantern became a black shape, crossing the snow towards the sheep, leaving footprints as deep as holes. He knew who it was. His father would be going to the sheltered field, making sure about the sheep. Martin felt a sudden impulse to go with him, knowing what a crisis snow could be. Then he remembered. He was different now. He could not hear when his father shouted.

He turned from the window and climbed the last three stairs, then along the landing to his room.

The light was already on. A hot-water bottle was

in the bed. A year ago he'd been contemptuous of hot-water bottles. Now it didn't matter. A second eiderdown had been added. His mother had done all this because now she did everything for him. She was trying to make amends.

He undressed quickly, feeling the snow making ghost shapes at the window. He put on his red and white pyjamas and hurried into bed, his feet reaching for the warmth made by the bottle. He snuggled down, congratulating himself because he was out of the cold. His bed seemed the warmest place in the world. He felt sorry for anyone out on a night like this. That was the first time he remembered. He remembered the pony in the orchard, then brushed the thought away.

Nothing to do with me. I never asked for it, never promised to look after it. Besides, it'll be all right. A Dartmoor pony must be used to snow.

His mother appeared, coming slowly into the room so that he would not look up suddenly and be startled. She tucked him up, tightening the covers around his shoulders. She made sure he was looking at her. Then she said, 'It's snowing thick.'

She turned out the light, leaving the landing light so that he would not be alarmed in the night. This was another change. Last winter he would have denied any suggestion that he was afraid of the dark. Now it was different. Now he needed to see because he could not hear.

He waited for his father to come up. He wanted to ask about the snow, the sheep, but guilt prevented him. He remembered how he had hurt his father with that long glare. His father went into the big bedroom. Martin felt the house settle down for the night. Only the landing light was still awake.

He tried to sleep. Sleep droned in the front of his mind, but the back of his mind was still awake. He couldn't forget the pony. He kept seeing pictures. He tried to say, not mine, I never promised. Martin screwed up his eyes, telling the pictures to go away. But the pictures were still there. He saw the snow crusting the pony's head and back, making its mane as wet as rain. He kept seeing its dejection because nobody cared.

He opened his eyes, looking at the wall-paper but not seeing the pattern. He was looking at the truth. He did care. This little pony needed him because it had nobody else. Every animal needed someone. Then he felt the wind. It shook the house, billowing the curtains. It tried to get in. He knew what the wind would do. It would carry the snow in white clouds, making drifts so deep you could drown. It wasn't snow alone which frightened the people of Dartmoor. It was wind and snow together, the one making drifts of the other. That was what covered sheep and cattle. That was what buried ponies.

Martin moved. He was out of bed so suddenly that the cold didn't matter. He scrambled into his clothes, adding two sweaters and a second pair of socks. He crept from the room and down the stairs. He was tense, knowing that his mother would stop him. In the passage he found his duffel coat. His gum boots were in a corner.

He found the switch of the kitchen, then moved to the door. He inched back the bolts, remembering what a noise they made. He opened the door and caught his breath, fighting to breathe. Then he remembered what the doctors had said and reached for a scarf. He must protect his ears. The doctors were always on about his ears. He tied the scarf around his head, then pulled up the hood of his duffel coat and opened the door again. The wind was waiting for him.

It drove snow at his face. He tasted it. He blinked to get it out of his eyes. He crept out, afraid that the dogs in the barn would hear and would start barking.

He could not open the yard gate. The drift was too deep. So he climbed the gate and when he stepped down to the other side, his boot went in almost to the top. He hesitated, knowing that if it was so deep here, it would be above his knees in the lane. Then he hurried.

His boots went deeper and deeper. His nose and eyes and mouth were frozen. Flakes blinded his eyelashes. They stuck to his eyelids like those shiny things which you stick on the eylids of the Demon King in pantomime.

He bowed his head to the wind, butting into it, showing the wind that although he was deaf now, different now, he was still strong enough.

His scarf became loose. It dragged from his neck, then fell, but he didn't bother to look for it.

He reached the gate of the orchard. He could see nothing, only a white curtain. He called, then realized that calling was no use. The wind took it away. Besides, he didn't even know the pony's name. Perhaps it had never been given a name.

He climbed the gate and groped towards the first tree. It leaned to grab, its branches as sharp as witch fingers. He could not see the pony. He fell so often that falling became part of moving forward. It didn't matter. He forgot that his boots were filled, that the front of his coat was white with snow which the wind was already freezing. The orchard seemed bigger than it had ever seemed in daylight.

He realized that the pony might be making distress sounds which he couldn't hear. He stumbled faster, his hands out, looking for the pony like the hands of the blind.

He was almost on top of it before he realized. He stopped, then came forward slowly, saying all the nice words in his head. The pony didn't move. Its head was down. Its back was thick with white. Its mane was as wet as rain. At first his fingers felt only the wetness. Then he felt something different, something hard and sharp. His fingers flinched. Icicles were already forming in its mane.

He took the forelock which fell between its ears. He moved towards where he imagined the gate to be, begging the pony to come.

The pony would not come. It looked into the wind, trying to find the place where the moor would be when light came. It seemed to think the moor was where it belonged.

Martin tried to say, you must come. Your mane will be all ice by the morning.

The pony stood a long time, still facing where the moor must be. Then it decided. It plodded after him, down the snow towards the gate.

Martin could not find the gate. There was a moment of panic. Then he thought, I mustn't panic, I must work it out. He stood in the ghost darkness, working it out. If he followed his own foot-holes, he must finally reach the gate.

But it wasn't as easy as that. His foot-holes were deceptive. He had wandered, so the foot-holes wandered. Sometimes the holes stopped suddenly, already smudged out by the wind.

Martin took a long time to find the gate. He lifted the gate from its hinges, dragging it back to make a gap. He got the pony through.

For two strides the little Dartmoor tried to run, but its legs sank too deep. Martin took its forelock again and led it down the lane.


Mrs. Manningham awoke first. She listened to the wind. It screamed around the house. It was a terrifying sound. It made her small inside.

She was afraid the wind had fingers and would tear away the roof. Then she heard the dogs.

At first she thought, it's nothing, they're being fools. But their persistence told her there must be something.

She thought at once that a prisoner had escaped from Princetown. This was the first fear of people who lived in the lonely places of the moor. They knew that an escaping prisoner would look for shelter, then food and clothes.

Perhaps a prisoner on the run was trying to get into a barn. Perhaps that's why the dogs were barking.

She nudged her husband, and reached for the bedside lamp. The sudden light took away some of her alarm. But the dogs were still barking.

Mr. Manningham awoke, screwing up his eyes from the lamp. He made a groaning noise.

'Listen,' she said.

He listened. At first he heard the wind and thought she was frightened by what the wind would do. Then he heard the dogs.

His wife said, 'Somebody in the yard. Somebody trying to get in.'

He made a sound of disbelief, but no moorland farmer could afford to ignore his dogs. They were telling him something. By the time he was out of bed he shared her fear that the 'somebody' was an escaped prisoner.

Poor fellow, out on a night like this. The sympathy was instinctive. It didn't last. He knew that any prisoner on the run might be dangerous, that his first duty was to protect his wife and son.

He was dressed in less than a minute. He hesitated at the top of the stairs, realizing that the 'somebody' might have already broken in; might be waiting for him in the darkness. Mr. Manningham bunched his fist and looked at it. It would do for a start.

He went down the stairs and into the passage. Only raincoats and gumboots. His gun was in a corner. He snatched it up, comforted by its smooth feel. It wasn't loaded. The shells were in the parlour, locked in a desk for safety. But no intruder would know that. One look at the gun might be enough.

The farmer pushed open the kitchen door. Nothing happened. His fingers groped for the switch. The sudden light showed there was no one.

Yet still the dogs were barking.

He pulled on a coat and stuffed his feet into gumboots. He passed through the kitchen and reached for the bolts.

They were already back. Somebody had gone out.

There was a moment of incredulity, for who would go out on a night like this? Then a cry on the landing told him.

'Martin,' his wife cried. 'His bed's empty. Martin's gone.'

Mr. Manningham couldn't believe it. He came to the bottom of the stairs, looking up to her distress.

He said, 'Gone where?'

It was a silly question. She came down, glancing for the duffel coat, to the corner where the boy's boots should be.

'He's outside,' she said. 'Somewhere in this.'

Mr. Manningham put down the gun. He seized his torch, checking it once. He dragged the door open and ducked out. The barking of the dogs was frenzied.

He hurried across the yard, opening the door of the barn. The dogs came out, bounding with excitement. He shouted and they came around, eager to please. He had hoped that perhaps they would find him. Now he saw it was hopeless. They were sheep dogs, not trained to track by smell.

He remembered the orchard. It was a faint hope, but perhaps. ... He climbed the gate to the lane. There were foot-holes, already filling. The boy had come this way.

But the foot-holes were too many, more than one boy could have made. He told himself, there were several of them. Several boys. It sounded incredible. He saw something. The end of a scarf, already stiff with ice. He recognized it as Martin's. He stuffed it into a pocket and pressed forward to the orchard.

The gate was down. He thought the boy must be in the orchard and shouted, forgetting that Martin could not hear. He shone his torch, flashing signals. But the snow came to the torch like moths to a light, fogging the glass in a minute.

He blundered into the orchard, searching it. There were foot-holes, crossing and criss-crossing, as though the boy had wandered like the lost.

Mr. Manningham staggered back towards the farm, trying to run, then falling and trying again. He reached the yard gate.

The dogs were still there. The young one was running around, sure this was some kind of game. But the old dog was wiser. He knew there was someone in the small shed which had been the harness-room in the days of horses.

It barked, showing the farmer where the someone was. Mr. Manningham couldn't believe it. Nothing was kept in the small shed. Only a few bales of straw.

At first he thought the old dog was a fool. Then he saw foot-holes leading to the shed. He went to the door and opened it. He flashed his torch, and the beam chanced on a flick of tail.

The pony was there, squeezed between bales of straw. It had its back to the door. Its ears were flattened, showing it had heard more than the boy.

The beam wandered and found Martin. He was standing at the pony's head, his eyes big with fright because he hadn't heard the dogs, hadn't heard his father. For him the torch was as sudden as a sword.

At first the father's alarms came out in anger. He wanted to say, 'Where you been? Frightening us like that.' The he came into the shed, putting a hand on the pony's quarters. The snow was melting. A wedge of it slipped down.

He looked to the boy and saw the white face, the shivering. Suddenly he understood what had happened in the orchard.

From the porch Mrs. Manningham called, 'What's happened? Have you found him?'

Farmer Manningham smiled, saying something in the smile which words could never say.

He had found his son, all right.

# CHAPTER THREE

THE farm was isolated. The radio reported heavy drifts. Snow-ploughs and bulldozers were trying to open moorland roads.

Martin watched his parents' faces as they listened. No newspapers could get through, so they were dependent on the radio. Their faces were anxious. Isolation meant the problems of getting out the churns of milk.

But Martin was relieved. For him isolation meant no school, and no school meant all day building a loose-box for the pony. He thought he could make it out of the old brown stable, where horses had stood in stalls in the old days. Knock down a wooden partition, then put up another wall and a door. That was the plan.

Last night, when he had thought it out, he had supposed that Nathan or his father would help. But Nathan and his father were already busy, shovelling a way out for the tractor and the milk churns.

He found a crowbar and heavy hammer. He took off his coat and swung the hammer, breaking down the partition. He prised with the crowbar. Soon his hands hurt. He wanted to give up, but he couldn't let the pony stay much longer in the narrow shed.

His mother crossed the yard to find him. She looked cold. Her shoulders were hunched. Martin was surprised that anyone could be cold. His sweat was itching like flies. He guessed she was telling him to come in.

'Nathan will help tomorrow. You can't do it alone.'

Martin wanted to do as much as possible alone. He wanted to show Nathan and his father. He leaned all his weight on the crowbar, forcing the old oak to give up the position it had occupied for a hundred years.

His mother said, 'You'll strain yourself.'

The partition crashed down at last, making a space wide enough for the pony to turn round. He used some of the wood to make another wall. He sawed it in measured lengths, but the saw was old and the wood was oak and soon his right arm was ready to drop off.

'You'll never do it,' his mother said.

He rested the wood on an empty oil-drum and knelt on it and sawed again. The old wood was not enough, so he climbed to the loft where the new wood was kept. The ladder was upright, like a ship's ladder. It had two staves missing. He scrambled up, as quick as a monkey. He found the planks of yellow wood and slid them down the hatch. This wood was soft. The saw bit easily. He sawed five pieces to the correct length, then found long nails and hammered the planks from one upright post to another. The stone walls made two sides of the box. The planks made another.

His mother came again, reminding him of

dinner. He didn't want to stop, even for half an hour, but she insisted. He followed her indoors and they had big plates of stew. He liked the potatoes and carrots and meat, but not the small dumplings. There was always a tussle about whether he should eat the dumplings. Years ago his father had said, 'They'll put hair on your chest,' and he'd believed it until he was six.

His father did not come to dinner. Martin understood he was still somewhere between the farm and the moorland road, cutting a way out. Every day milk churns had to be taken by trailer to the junction with the moorland road. That was where the lorry from the milk depot collected them.

Martin felt the drag of the fire. Tiredness and warmth made his legs and arms heavy. He began to drowse, telling himself there was no need to hurry, the pony could wait.

Then he straightened, shaking sleep away, knowing that if he didn't leave the fire now, he would waste the afternoon. He went back to his work, hoping to get much of it done before his father and Nathan came back.

The easy part had been done. Now he must make a door. It had seemed simple enough in his head. Two parallel pieces, then a diagonal, and nail the planks to them. But soon he admitted that his door was not working out. At first he thought, never mind, it'll do. Then he imagined what his father would say, and ripped out the nails and began again.

'Here,' Nathan said. 'Let's give a hand.'

Martin was surprised that Nathan was back. He

26

stood aside, letting the farm-hand take over,
hoping his father would never know what a mess
he'd made of it.

But Nathan could help only for an hour. After
that he had other work to do and Martin was alone
again.

He didn't know he was talking to himself. He
said aloud, 'I've got to get it finished – before Dad
comes to look.'

He found the hinges and hunted for screws.
Shepherds Hill kept screws and bolts in a red tin
which had once been used for sweets. You tipped
out the contents, not really expecting to find what
you wanted. But somehow you always did. Then
you scooped back the rest and replaced the tin
above the beam, where the cobwebs were.

Martin put in the screws. He liked this sort of
work. It was work which the deaf could do as well
as those who could hear. It was kind work. It didn't
make you feel stupid because you couldn't hear.
The screws went easily into the new wood, but
when he tried to attach the flange of each hinge to
the oak post, the old wood won. He drilled deeper
holes, but still the screws wouldn't turn.

His father saw the struggling and spent half an
hour helping to fix the hinges and to hang the door.
They watched the door swing. Martin kept swing-
ing it, proud and rather surprised. He darted a grin
and his father winked.

But it wasn't finished yet. Martin screwed on
bolts, one at the top, another at the bottom, using
two because a bored pony might rattle back one.
After that he fixed the wooden crib. It hadn't been

used for years, except by the barn cat which had kittens in it. He put a wooden leg under the end that tilted, lifting it with his back while he forced in the leg. The crib was heavy. Everything old was heavy. The pain in his back seemed like going on for ever.

'Surely you've done enough now,' his mother said.

He switched on the light. The bulb was high and pale. It seemed not to be powerful enough, but it strengthened as daylight faded.

He cleaned the crib, scraping out the dust of years. Then he brought bran in a bucket and tipped it in. The pony could not have oats. Sudden oats would inflame its legs. But bran was not heating. It would do no harm and would be a change from hay or grass. He stuffed hay into the rack above the crib, then brought in straw for the earth floor. He fluffed it up with a pitch-fork, billowing it like a yellow sea. The straw gave the box a homely look, like putting down a carpet in a house.

He looked around, admiring what he had done. It wasn't an ideal box. Not like the boxes you read about in textbooks. But it had been made with few materials. It was better than most ponies ever saw.

He went out to the yard, surprised by the darkness, by the bustle of milking in the shippen. He hadn't realized it was so late.

He opened the door of the narrow shed which had been good enough last night but would never be good enough again. The pony's tail swished, telling him that it was bored. It wanted to get out.

It came out backwards, its head alert, trembling and suspicious. Martin held its fore-lock, persuading it towards the loose-box. It went in. It looked around and puffed the straw. It didn't seem to be impressed. Then it found the crib, the bran, and suddenly it was convinced. It plunged in its nose. It ate with concentration, thinking about nothing else, reminding Martin of the fat boy at school who never looked up until his plate was empty.

Martin laughed and the pony looked up briefly. Its nose was spattered with bran, like brown sawdust. He laughed again, delighted by the comedy. In that moment it ceased to be an 'it'. It became somebody. It had a name.

'Tuppence,' he said, finding the name in his head.

It seemed a good name. He said it over and over, waiting for its ears to twitch in answer.

He looked around, startled by the shadow. His father came into the box, looking around, making sure the work had been done well. He gave the pony a slap.

'Tuppence,' Martin said.

His father nodded. Good name, easy to remember.

Now Martin wanted to know everything. He asked so many questions that Mr. Manningham let most of them go, answering only those of which he was sure.

'She's a filly, three years old. She's never had a foal.'

Harvey hadn't been able to sell her, although

she'd been on trial four times. Each time she'd been returned as unsuitable.

'Too nervous,' Mr. Manningham said. 'Imagining ghosts round every corner.'

He laughed, making a joke of it, but Martin didn't think it was a joke. Perhaps Tuppence did see more than any human being could. Nobody knew what a horse or pony saw or heard. Martin thought this nervousness was a sign of her intelligence.

He looked up as his father touched his shoulder.

'Time we were in,' Mr. Manningham said. 'Your mother's waiting supper.'

They went out of the box. Martin closed the bolts and tip-toed for a last look. She had finished the bran. She was tearing hay from the rack, stuffing it in as though afraid the feast wouldn't last.

'Tuppence,' he said.

She looked around. Hay hung from both sides of her mouth, like the whiskers of a television comic.

She wagged the whiskers as she chewed, her eyes big and serious, wondering why he was laughing.

He was still laughing as he walked beside his father.

There was more snow in the night. When Martin looked from his window, he could not see the track which his father and Nathan had cut to get the milk out.

The moor was built up into false shapes. There were no crevices, no valleys, no walls. What seemed to be lines of granite were the top stones of walls. The rest was buried.

He dressed hurriedly and ran to the yard. Nathan and his father were shovelling paths to the barns and shippen. He helped by digging a path to the stable.

Tuppence moved around her box, looking for hay. The water in her bucket was frozen. The ice was as thick as glass. Martin gave her more food, more water, then went back to the war against snow. Mr. Manningham was trying to get the tractor and trailer down the slope to the bridge. He liked to boast that the old tractor would get anywhere in any weather, but it couldn't get through snow as deep as this. Martin helped dig it out. They tried again, and again it failed.

Despairingly Mr. Manningham said, 'We'll have to wait for a thaw.'

There was no thaw. A freezing wind hardened the snow and made it seem as permanent as stone. The line of milk churns grew until all the spare churns were used. Martin knew how serious it was. Shepherds Hill was a mixed farm, with sheep and pigs and bullocks as well as milking cows. But the most important product was milk. If the farm could not sell its milk, it would soon be bankrupt.

'Not your fault,' Mrs. Manningham said. 'Nobody could get through snow like this.'

But Mr. Manningham knew that somehow he must get through. All his milk went to the milk depot. It was his responsibility to get it to the highway for collection. The longer he failed the more milk would be wasted. None of it would be paid for.

Martin saw him on the telephone, knowing from the anger and anxiety that he was talking to the milk depot, trying to explain. But the milk depot had its own problems. All its lorries were out, trying to pick up the milk at collecting points. All its drivers were struggling through blizzards deeper than anyone could remember.

'I'm too far from the road,' Mr. Manningham said. 'The tractor can't get out.'

The voice at the other end made a sympathetic noise. Then it said, 'The lorry will be your way about three o'clock today. Try to get out as much as you can.'

The farmer's anxiety became a shout of rage. 'I keep telling you. There's snow eight feet deep shutting us in.'

He slammed down the phone, then looked at his wife. Martin saw their tired bewilderment.

He went to the yard, but this time he did not help his father and Nathan make desperate attempts with the tractor. He found wood and nails and screws. He'd had an idea. It might work. He could see no reason why it shouldn't. But he wasn't ready to tell his father yet. He knew what happened to good ideas. Often they broke down half-way.

This one didn't. He showed it to his father. A sledge, see. Put traces on Tuppence and harness her to the sledge and draw the churns across the snow. His father waved away the idea. It wouldn't work, the snow would crack. The sledge would capsize, spilling the churns, or the pony would kick, not used to working in harness. But the more he considered it, the more the chance seemed worth taking.

'After all,' he told his wife, 'it's better than doing nothing and if it does work, we're saved.'

He strengthened Martin's sledge, adding long screws instead of nails. He put hooks and ropes on either side, with ropes to tie the churns.

Nathan loaded them. Each was of eight gallons and weighed over a hundredweight.

'Try three,' the farmer said. 'Three the first time. Then if it works, we can try more the second.'

Martin brought the pony out. He fastened the traces, telling Tuppence what it was all about and why it was so important. He felt sure the pony understood. But his mother saw only a quick-tempered pony, flattening its ears and swishing its tail, suspicious of the weight at its heels.

She said, 'Don't you go. It's no work for a boy.'

Martin shook his head. He would go because Tuppence was his pony.

He looked to his father, waiting for a signal that the churns were roped and safe. Then he took the bridle and spoke. Tuppence moved forward. Then she stopped, surprised by the weight behind her. She looked back. Her expression was indignant.

Martin laughed, although his mother could see nothing to laugh about. Patiently he explained it all again. Tuppence answered with a kick.

'There,' his mother cried. 'I told you. One kick could break your leg.'

Martin stumbled as his father pushed him aside. Mr. Manningham's patience was frayed. He had eighty gallons to get out and no pony was going to stop him.

He took the bridle and dragged. Tuppence stiffened her forelegs and glared. He shouted for his whip.

Tuppence heard the first crack. It exploded like a pistol shot. She didn't go forward. She darted sideways, tangling a leg in the trace and fighting to be free.

Martin did not hear the crack, but he saw what it did to his pony. He shouted. His father hesitated, surprised by the boy's white fury.

Then he said, 'This isn't a game. The pony must be made to go.'

But Nathan murmured, 'Let the boy try his way.'

Mr. Manningham hesitated, then stood back. He and Nathan stood with Mrs. Manningham, watching Martin talking to the pony.

For ten minutes nothing happened. Every time Martin asked her to come forward, Tuppence stiffened her forelegs and held up her head, looking at him in defiance.

Martin shook his head, reproaching, making her ashamed. He was sure she understood much more than adults believed possible. He was sure that sooner or later she'd give in to get it over.

His father turned away with a despairing sound. In that instant Tuppence moved forward.

'Look,' Nathan said.

When the farmer looked over a shoulder the sledge was moving. He let out a cheering sound, waving encouragement as the boy looked back.

Martin recognized the signs of encouragement. He was applauding every step, making every step an achievement, assuring her that if only she could keep the sledge moving, there would be no reward big enough. He thought she would make it to the bridge. Then she found the loose snow which the tractor had broken. She tried to struggle, but he knew she'd never do it.

He looked back. His father was hurrying to help.

Mr. Manningham stooped, a hand on the pony's leg. He bent it and lifted, showing Martin the hoof. Loose snow was balled inside the hoof, crippling her attempts to walk. He looked at all her feet, then shouted to the house.

Martin was bewildered. There seemed nothing his father could do. The attempt seemed doomed.

He didn't hear his mother answer, 'What did you say?'

'Butter. Butter or margarine. As much as you can spare.'

Nathan brought it. The farmer plucked snow from the hooves and smeared in butter and margarine. It seemed a waste of food. Martin was shocked. His father never wasted anything. Then he saw what the grease was doing. It was padding the hooves, keeping them free of snow.

Mr. Manningham gave Tuppence back the last foot, then watched her try again. She struggled, but this time the loose snow did not cripple. He and Nathan leaned their strength into the churns behind. The sledge moved and kept moving until

Martin's shout said they had reached the firm snow on the other side.

'Keep her going,' Mr. Manningham panted, forgetting that Martin could not hear.

Martin kept her going with flattery and promises. A bowl of bran with a few oats sprinkled. That was the equivalent of winning the penny points. Well, she'd have the equivalent of a first dividend if only she got there and proved to everyone what she could do.

But the promises ran out half-way, not because he couldn't think of any, but because he had no breath. His hands and face were frozen, but within his woollens his body was hot. He felt sweat itching inside the waistband of his trousers. It seemed absurd that anyone could be so cold and so hot at the same time.

Then he thought of something and looked back to the farm, where black figures were watching. He knew they were his parents and Nathan. He wanted to tell them that even if he reached the road, it would not be enough.

'The churns,' his thoughts said. 'They'll have to be lifted off and how can I do that?'

Almost he stopped, ready to give in because no boy could lift a hundredweight. Then other thoughts pushed him forward. Mustn't give in, there must be a way. He found it. He would dig away the snow with his hands, making a platform behind the sledge. Then he would waggle each churn to it, not lifting at all. He thought he could waggle a hundredweight quite easily.

He reached the ridge and looked down. A

snow-plough was crawling, as small as a beetle. Men were shovelling. They were keeping the road open for the milk lorry.

Tuppence snorted, her breath like kettle puffs. They came down the slope. Martin walked in front, testing the surface, a hand reaching back for the reins. Tuppence stepped where he stepped, nervous of going downhill because of the weight behind. Their descent was slow.

The workmen saw them and shouted questions, then exchanged glances because the boy did not answer. They shouted louder and still he did not answer. Then they shrugged because if he didn't want to answer ...

Martin brought the sledge to a section which the snowplough had cleared. He began to dig with his hands. The foreman shouted, 'What you up to?' But still the boy didn't answer. The men watched him straighten from the digging, then struggle with a churn. The weight was more, much more than he'd expected. He couldn't do it. He stopped for a breather, then tried again, but still he couldn't do it.

The foreman muttered, 'What's he up to?' and came forward. He was talking to himself as he approached. 'Out of the way, son, you'll strain yourself.'

But the boy didn't seem to know he was coming. When he reached the sledge and touched him, the boy jumped in fright. The pony felt the boy's fright and lurched sideways, dragging the sledge and almost toppling the churns. The foreman shouted and the men ran to help. One held the pony while others heaved the churns upright. They looked at the foreman above the boy's head.

'He's deaf,' the foreman said.

The men were surprised. Then they lifted the churns, struggling them to the platform which Martin had made. It was done in a minute.

The foreman touched Martin's hands, pressing open first one hand, then the other. They were cut and bruised, showing how hard and sharp the snow had been. The tips of the fingers were bleeding. Martin was surprised. He hadn't felt any pain and still didn't. He guessed the pain would come when he held his hands to a fire.

The foreman beckoned with a movement of his head. He opened his flask and poured hot tea. He held out the cup. It was tea without milk. It was strong and sweet. He spoke carefully, so that Martin could see. 'Drink – it'll do you good.' Then he asked, 'You going back for more?'

'If there's time,' Martin answered.

The foreman took out his watch, showing it to make sure the boy understood. It was nearly half-past one.

'There might be time,' Martin said. 'If the lorry's late.'

He held the cup between both hands. He lifted it to sip again, but a nose jolted his elbow, spilling the tea. He looked around in surprise. Tuppence was nudging, suggesting a share.

The men laughed. One reached for his dinner-bag and brought out a sandwich. He broke it and Tuppence grabbed. There was nothing suspicious about her now. She ate like the starving, then peered round for more. All the men brought pieces from their bags; the pieces which they had been saving for an afternoon snack. They made a pet of her and in a few minutes Tuppence mixed cheese sandwich with cherry cake and pastry and buttered scones. Martin doubted that she tasted any of it.

He gave back the cup, smiling to show that he appreciated. Then he reached for the reins, persuading Tuppence from the petting of the men. She didn't want to come. She liked their flattery. They laughed at her reluctance, holding out their tins, their dinner-bags, showing there was nothing left. Tuppence was incredulous. But when she was sure they had nothing left, she turned without a backward glance, washing her hands of them.

Martin laughed, shaking his head at such ingratitude. Tuppence showed no remorse. She hurried up the hill, realizing that she was going home and that home meant something good.

When they reached the ridge, Martin looked down and waved. The workmen answered. There was a moment of deep friendliness on the frozen moor.

These men had become part of the struggle to get the milk out. He would never know their names, might never see them again. But he would never forget.

Mrs. Manningham was watching the ridge. She saw the black movement and called her husband from the shippen. They stayed at the gate a long time, watching the boy and pony come home.

'You shouldn't let him,' Mrs. Manningham said.

'It's too dangerous. You know he'll never be like other boys.'

But Mr. Manningham laughed. His pride exploded in a shout.

He put an arm around her as he said, 'Shouldn't let him? His idea, his sledge, his pony. He'd never have forgiven me if I'd stopped him.'

He stayed near the gate until he was sure that boy and pony were safely home. Then he ran to the kitchen and grabbed the 'phone. He wanted to tell the depot, to tell someone, anyone. Telling would be a kind of celebration.

But the 'phone was dead. The line was down, broken by the blizzard. He looked towards the door as his wife came in with Martin. His shrug told them what had happened. He replaced the useless thing. There was a moment of fear in the kitchen.

Martin glanced from his father to his mother and back again. He saw what their fear was saying. The breakdown of the telephone was the end of their last link with the world. Now they were completely isolated. The radio could only tell them of what had happened to others. It could not warn others of crisis at Shepherds Hill. Whatever happened at Shepherds Hill, they would be on their own as long as the blizzard lasted.

# CHAPTER FOUR

THE electricity failed. Mrs. Manningham brought out lamps and candles, going back to life on the moor as it had been before the war. Martin liked the candles. The flames grew like flowers. The lamplight was mellow, leaving corners of the kitchen in the mystery of shadow. But the failure of electricity meant more than inconvenience in the house. It meant that the milking machine was useless. All milking had to be by hand. For Nathan this was going back to the old method. He preferred to milk by hand. It was more personal and every cow was different. But for Martin it was new. He had to learn.

Nathan started him with Lettuce, the oldest and most patient cow. He learned to drag his stool forward and tuck his head into the brown side and tilt the bucket between his knees, then to call down the milk in a white rain. The milk smelled warm. The barn cat crept to a spilled puddle. The cat's tongue made little ticking sounds. He remembered the sounds as he watched its furtive lapping. The cat was not supposed to be in the shippen. It was supposed to be unseen, hunting in the gloom of the barn, keeping down the mice and rats. No farmer pampered his barn cats, because the more he pampered the less they hunted. But the blizzard made its own rules. The cat needed somewhere warm. It also needed something to drink, for the water was frozen. Martin let it stay and Nathan pretended not to notice. Only when it heard the farmer's footsteps did the cat disappear, as swift as a shadow, hiding somewhere until it was safe again.

At first Martin had boasted to himself that before the end of a week, he would be milking as many as Nathan. It wasn't as easy as that. He was surprised by the pain in his fore-arms. His wrists ached. Lumps formed on the inside. He touched them and winced with pain.

'There's no need,' his mother protested. 'Your hands are still cut from scraping away the snow.'

But Martin liked helping. He liked the warmth of the cows and the smell of the milk and working with Nathan. But most of all he liked Lettuce. She had a personality no less than Tuppence, although quite different. Where Tuppence was a comedienne, always hungry, always looking for flattery, Lettuce was calm and distant, always dreaming. She thought a lot. Martin laughed, reminded of a hymn he used to sing. 'Let us with a gladsome mind . . .' In his thoughts he made it 'Lettuce with a gladsome mind', calling it her signature tune.

There was more snow, more wind. The news on the radio was all about the blizzard. There were reports of hundreds of sheep lost on the moor, of ponies starving, of the R.S.P.C.A. supplying hay by helicopter.

The radio became the most important thing in

43

the house. His parents sat near it, never missing a bulletin. His mother jotted down fragments of each bulletin, giving him scraps of paper to read because he could read the written word much easier than he could read lips.

'Ponies starving,' she wrote. Then added, 'Harvey's,' with several exclamation marks to show what she thought of Harvey. Martin felt their anger and understood it. They were angry with Harvey because their pride as Dartmoor farmers was hurt. No farmer should so neglect his stock that R.S.P.C.A. hay became necessary. Harvey had been warned many times, but he made no provisions. Each winter he took a chance with the weather, sure that if it was bad, the R.S.P.C.A. would feed his ponies for him. To Harvey it might have seemed very clever. It saved him money, for hay cost over twelve pounds a ton. But Martin knew what his father thought of it. Mr. Manningham was afraid that if the R.S.P.C.A. could prove neglect, the Government would take away the farmers' rights to graze animals on the moor.

If that happened, the Government wouldn't take away the right from Harvey only. That wouldn't be so bad. It would be a kind of justice. They would take it also from all the moorland farmers.

It was an old right, but old rights were not always safe in a world of change. There were always many who wanted to take away from others what they could not have themselves. Mr. Manningham was afraid that Harvey's neglect would give the Government an excuse to clear all animals off the moor.

Martin watched his father's face, guessing what was being said.

'Harvey's letting us all down. One Harvey can undo all the work ten others try to do.'

Day by day the radio informed them of cars lost, of parties marooned, of the valour of lorry-drivers in getting milk to the towns.

Then the voice said, 'One Dartmoor farm is getting out its milk by sledge, drawn by a Dartmoor pony.'

Martin saw his parents' astonishment. He watched his mother as she wrote, 'You – on the radio just now – Tuppence and the sledge.'

His surprise became a question. He saw that his parents shared it. Who could have told the B.B.C.? He thought for a minute. Then a face came into his mind. The foreman, that day on the road. He had told the reporter.

Later Martin told Tuppence about it. He said, 'You're famous,' and Tuppence hung her head in a bashful way, pretending to be overwhelmed.

As the blizzard dragged on, without hint of a thaw, the radio reported the plight of moorland farms. Many were without food or candles. Some were crying 'Help', using stones to print the word in the snow, hoping that helicopters would see.

At first there was no such crisis at Shepherds Hill. Mrs. Manningham prepared for winter as people in history prepared for a siege. The shelves of the big, whitewashed larder were heavy with tinned food, including soup and corned beef.

She bought coal in summer, when prices were low and supplies were plentiful. She made sure

45

there were drums of paraffin for lamps and lanterns. A lean-to shed was stuffed with logs, sawn by Nathan during wet days in September and October. All pipes were wrapped in sacking, with straw packed around those pipes where the risk was greatest. Every precaution was taken, for she knew how severe winter could be. But even she had not prepared for a blizzard as long as this.

The water supply froze. It had frozen before, but Nathan or Mr. Manningham had thawed the pipes and the taps had gushed again. This time it froze so that there was nothing they could do. To be without water for the house was bad enough. You realized how much water you used in a day only when you had to carry it. But to be without water for the farm was much worse.

A calf drank eight gallons a day. There were eleven calves. Cows and bullocks drank more and there were nearly forty.

The only sources were the well, which had not been used for years, and the stream which had been frozen for weeks. Nathan uncovered the well and got the windlass and bucket working. Martin and his father broke the ice of the stream with pickaxes, dipping their buckets to the water beneath.

The well supplied the house; the stream supplied the animals. Martin spent hours a day carrying water to the calves. They became his responsibility. They crowded around the metal barrel as he tipped the water in. Then down to the stream and back again to a barrel already empty.

Water was not the only anxiety. His mother was worried about paraffin and candles. The house must be kept lit and warm. She needed supplies from the store at the cross-roads. But the cross-roads were five miles away. Martin didn't want to go. He was sick of the snow. He hated it. He looked forward to the thaw and promised never again to grumble about sunshine and grass and heather, about roads you could see and move along.

His mother didn't ask him. She asked her husband. Mr. Manningham didn't want to go either. He was already busy from first light to last. So was Nathan. But he knew he must go.

They needed more than paraffin and candles. They needed matches, flour, salt, sugar, yeast for bread. The list was lengthening every day.

Martin didn't know what was happening until his father led Tuppence from her box. She was bridled, but had no saddle. The stirrups would be too short.

She came willingly to the gate, suspecting nothing. Mr. Manningham put a foot on the gate, then threw a leg across her back. He settled himself, waiting for his wife to bring the sack and list.

It was then Tuppence realized. Her indignation was comic. She looked round to the strange knee, the strange leg, the strange boot, further down than a boot should be. She waited for the strange weight to get off. Then she tried scorn. When that failed, she tried obstinacy.

'Giddup,' Mr. Manningham said.

He looked ridiculous, so tall a man on so small a pony. He knew it and the knowledge didn't improve his temper. He suspected the pony was about to buck him off. He shouted and moved his elbows, making it plain that she had to go.

Tuppence pretended to be thinking of other things. She looked round to Martin. The reproach was there for all to see. Even Nathan laughed, then glanced an apology to the farmer.

Martin hurried, shamed by the reproach. He touched his father's knee, asking to be allowed to go. His mother's hand was saying no, you mustn't, it's too far, but his father's predicament was the more urgent.

There was always the possibility that Tuppence would give in to her sense of humour. Martin could imagine his father sitting in the snow, humiliated for ever. He pulled his father's knee, begging him to do it the easy way.

Mr. Manningham hesitated long enough to prove that he was the equal of any half-pint pony. Then he got down, ignoring the little shrug with which Tuppence helped him.

'Too busy anyway,' he told his wife. 'It's best for the boy to go.'

Martin did not wait for a saddle. He put a hand on her wither, another on her rump, and jumped. She was moving before he struggled up. He turned her in an arc towards his mother.

'Mrs. Manningham passed the sack and shopping list. 'Here,' she said. 'The money.'

She gave him a purse. He opened it, took out four pounds and tucked the notes in an inner pocket. Then he gave back the purse. She didn't understand that boys never carried purses. She said, 'Be careful now. Don't lose the money now.'

Mr. Manningham held open the gate. Tuppence went by with a cheeky whisk of her tail, showing that he wasn't the boss of all the animals on the farm.

Her step was jaunty as they crossed the moor. She'd grown used to snow now, as though grass and earth and tarmac belonged to a world which would never come back. She gave little bucks of exuberance, telling him that she belonged to him, that she would be like this for nobody else.

He slapped her neck, delighted by this sense of partnership. They would do things together, as partners should. They'd go hunting, compete in gymkhanas and pony trials. They'd show Harvey what they could do.

He talked to her as they crossed the white face of the moor. He even sang, singing a remembered song because there was no one to hear. The moor was as empty as the moon.

He saw the store at the cross-roads. It seemed near, but he knew how deceptive distance could be on the moor. It was still two miles away. The store was popular in summer. Holiday cars drew up for petrol, for cigarettes and ice-cream. Grannie Webber hung out a sign saying 'Cream Teas' and touring families ate strawberries and cream beside the stepping-stones.

But summer seemed far away. The store was as isolated as an outpost of civilization in a wilderness. Its only customers were people from scattered farms and cottages, making perilous journeys for the means of staying alive.

Martin opened the door. He could not hear the

bell, but he remembered how it jangled. Grannie waited while he groped for the shopping list. His fingers were clumsy with cold. She did not speak until he was looking at her.

Then she said, 'How's things at home?'

'All right,' Martin answered.

Grannie glanced at the pencilled list. It told her more than the boy's 'all right'.

Mrs. Manningham wanted candles, which meant the electricity had failed at Shepherds Hill as it had failed at other farms. She also wanted tea and cocoa, which meant they were boiling water, not trusting the well.

Yeast, flour, matches, sugar. Grannie made a pile on the counter.

Then she saw the last item; margarine and butter, more than they could possibly need for bread and cooking. She thought his mother had made a mistake. She held out the list, pointing to it. The boy nodded, confirming that they wanted all that. He was going to explain about using margarine and butter in the pony's hooves. Then he stopped, partly because he was nervous of talking, chiefly because Grannie already knew too much.

Grannie liked to know all the local news; about who was getting married and who had passed the eleven-plus. Grown-ups called her 'a character'. Children thought she was 'nosy'.

Reluctantly she added the margarine and butter, sure that Shepherds Hill didn't know what it was doing. Then she said, 'Got a new pony then.'

This was an invitation for him to tell her all

about it, but Martin pretended he couldn't understand. He guessed that Grannie already knew too
much about Tuppence, even what his father had
paid for her.

Grannie ticked the list, sucking her pencil and
putting the price against each item. Her lips
moved, counting silently. She had left school at ten,
but she seldom made a mistake.

She wrote the total and showed it to Martin. He
put the notes on the counter and opened his sack,
putting in the stores. He waited for the change,
thinking there was nothing else. He had forgotten
the paraffin.

Grannie brought it from somewhere behind the
shop. The can had a handle. It was strongly corked.
She wired the cork so that jolting could not loosen
it. Her fingers were strong and deft, twisting the
wire like string. Her care with the wire made him
ashamed of the children's name for her.

She wasn't only 'nosy'. She wanted Shepherds
Hill to get its paraffin safely. Seventy winters on the
moor had taught her how important paraffin could
be.

Martin knew he should have remembered the
can, the wire for the cork. He decided never to call
her 'nosy' again, especially when she was.

Grannie asked, 'How you going to carry it?'

She meant the can as well as the sack. Martin
showed her with his hands, preferring gestures because they were less strain than talking. The can on
one side, the bag on the other.

Grannie nodded and stooped. When she straightened she had a length of rope. She made quick

loops, tying the handle of the can to the sack with a short length of rope between.

He saw the sense of it and thanked her. Sack and can were heavy. He struggled to get through the door. The cold seemed colder because of the warmth in the store.

Tuppence was eating something in the middle of the hedge. She had nudged away the snow to find it. He hung the sack on one side of her wither, the can on the other. She looked over a shoulder with what amounted to a frown, then admitted this was no time for argument. She tore at whatever she had found in the middle of the hedge. She chewed the twigs with relish.

Martin struggled back, glancing to Grannie's face at the window. He raised a hand, then turned towards the moor.

For a minute Tuppence moved grudgingly, sucking her teeth in a thoughtful way, still remembering the twigs. Then she realized she was going home and quickened to a trot.

Martin looked down, making sure the snow did not ball in her feet. Nathan had told him it was safe to trot in snow so thick. Even race-horses, with precious legs, could be safely cantered in thick snow.

Looking down showed him the birds. A tuft of feathers here, another there. So many dead that he wondered if there would be any birds to celebrate the spring. Even a snipe, hardiest of marsh-birds. He recognized its carcass. The wind had not yet plucked its feathers. He guessed it had died only recently. Perhaps an hour ago, when he had passed this way towards the store, it had been still clinging to the magic called life.

Tuppence felt the tug of home and her trot took on a merry rhythm. He felt the power in her.

She was only 12.2 hands in a straight line from the wither. Each hand was four fingers, and each finger was an inch. This meant she was only fifty inches high. But her back was broad. Her neck was thick. Her quarters were wide and strong.

This power was now dedicated to getting home. Not before had he realized how fast and brave she could be when the mood was right. He delighted in it. He didn't hear the sound in the sky.

Tuppence heard it. She flattened her ears and ducked sideways, almost throwing him. The sound came lower and suddenly the strength which had been dedicated to getting home, became hostile, a coiled spring which tightened and leaped, first this way, then that.

He clung and shouted, worried about the paraffin. He felt the wind, as sudden as a whirlwind. He looked up, but saw nothing.

Tuppence bucked. He had neither saddle nor stirrups. He could not hold on. He began to fall. The white blow rushed up and exploded in his face.

Martin tried to open his eyes. The corners were stuck. He realized they were stuck with ice. His fright fought them open. Then he lay a moment, looking at the snow.

He remembered and struggled up. One side of

his face was crusted. He back-handed the snow away, looking for Tuppence.

She had gone. He saw her footprints, going up the hill towards home. Then he remembered the sack, the paraffin, and saw them a few yards away.

He moved towards them, but his legs would not respond. They staggered drunkenly. He began to fall. His hands could not save him. The jolting blow was in his head again.

He knew he must get up, that if he did not the wind would come for him. He told his legs and arms to fight. They were as dead as wood.

His thoughts became tired. He wanted to sleep. It was good sense to lie and sleep. The snow seemed as comfortable as a bed.

He felt himself going over the edge to sleep. Dimly he was aware that the whirlwind was back, pressing him down. It didn't matter. Nothing could keep him from sleep.

Then a strong arm was around him. He felt his father's rough cheek, smelled his father's tobacco smell. He tried to explain, she was coming home merrily, she took me by surprise.

For a while the whirlwind was furious above them. Then it moved away and the cold stillness came back. Martin forced his eyes open. The snow seemed as white as a great, unmade bed. His father's arm was persuading him to walk.

He moved a pace or two before he remembered. He looked to where the sack and can had been. Nathan was there, holding the can in one hand, the sack in the other.

Martin thought, that's all right then. He remembered Grannie wiring the cork. Only the wire had held the cork in. If Grannie had not helped, the paraffin would have splashed and there'd have been nothing for the lamps.

His father helped him up the hill. It seemed a long way, longer than it had ever been. Each time he opened his eyes, he saw only snow. He tried to ask about Tuppence. Where was she? Was she all right, and why had she done it?

We were partners. I felt sure she'd never hurt me. So why?

He thought he was speaking aloud, but the thoughts were only in his head. Not until he was in bed, with his mother near, did the word get out of his head and into the room.

Then he said, 'Why?' Over and over, showing her how important it was.

His parents tried to tell him but he could not understand because his eyes were closed. He stayed in the red fog of delirium until the following day.

Even when he got his eyes open, he could not concentrate long enough to read her lips or understand her gestures. He slept again and when he awoke, he was stronger.

She had it ready, written on a pad. The words were in block letters, making it easy. 'Helicopter frightened the pony ...'

There was more but the words blurred as he tried to read them. They were not important. He had found out what he wanted most to know.

Not her fault, he thought, as he drifted again into

the red sea of sleep. She had not thrown him out of malice.

The next day he learned the rest. The helicopter had come directly above, looking for Harvey's ponies. It had made the whirlwind. He had felt it but could not hear.

Tuppence had come home in a sweat of fright. For a while his father had not known where to look. Then the helicopter had hovered above the farm, signalling that the pilot knew.

The machine had led Mr. Manningham and Nathan to the boy on the other side of the hill. It had hovered long enough to make sure he was all right. Then his father had signalled and it had moved on, still looking for animals to feed.

Mr. Manningham and Nathan had got him home. He had been delirious, with a temperature of 103. Now his temperature was down. His eyes were cool and he saw his parents clearly. The only sign of his fall was a bruise on a cheek-bone.

The next day he came down to the firelit kitchen. His father brought Tuppence to the window, beckoning Mrs. Manningham to open it.

She complained about the cold, but he insisted. Tuppence put in her head, ears sharp with curiosity, eyes alight with greed like a glutton coming to a birthday-party table. Martin broke a crust and held out the pieces, laughing as she grabbed.

He touched her nostrils. They were as tender as the inside of a flower. He said, 'It was me. My fault. I didn't hear a thing.'

He pressed against her smell, combing the

tangled mane with his fingers. She nudged for more bread and Martin gave it.

He said, 'I knew you wouldn't do it on purpose. I knew you'd never hurt me.'

# CHAPTER FIVE

THE snow thawed. The white mask slipped away, slowly, then suddenly, showing the old moor beneath.

For a while the moor was haggard, exhausted by the cruel winter. Then it began to straighten, to take an interest in itself, like an old man recovering from a long illness.

It began to remember that the time was spring. First a bud of gorse, as yellow as a guardsman's button. Then a bird. Then a lamb, dragging milk from a ewe still gaunt beneath its heavy wool.

Martin counted the signs of spring. It was the season of transformation. Every year the same magic, yet every year he was startled by it.

He wanted to say, 'It's wonderful. You'd never believe that a fortnight ago, all this was deep in snow.'

He glanced to his father as the car sped towards the city. His father understood the glance and nodded to the sturdy lambs.

'They look good, better than you'd expect.'

There was a sense of rejoicing in the car. It seemed that spring was a kind of triumph, that cruel winter had been defeated.

They left the wild moor for city streets, for shops

and 'buses and elaborate traffic signs. Office girls were hurrying to work. Men had newspapers under their arms. Schoolboys on bicycles were as thick as starlings.

Martin looked past them, pretending not to see. They reminded him how different he had become. Once he had gone to their type of school. He had been among the starlings. Now he went to a special school. Now he was not allowed to ride a bike. His parents were fearful of him attempting to cross a busy road. Now he was as helpless in traffic as someone old and doddering.

The car drew near the special school. He still could not think of it as his school, could not believe that he would be here until he was sixteen. He still wanted to think of it as temporary, that soon whatever had happened to his ears would be put right and he would hear again.

The car stopped. Others were going into the school. They were in pairs, in groups of three or four. They were laughing. You couldn't believe they were deaf.

Martin saw that they had no resentment. That was their secret. They accepted their deafness as a fact which nothing could change. They were learning to live with it.

His father wanted him to be like that. But I can't, Martin thought, I still hope. It seemed easier for them because they were born deaf.

Then he saw the little girl, coming towards the school with her mother. The little girl had blue eyes and golden hair. She was three years old and had been born deaf.

Martin looked down at the little girl. A minute ago he had told himself it was easier for 'them' because they had never listened. Now he knew better. It was never easy.

He smiled and the girl answered. He got out and closed the door, with a quick glance to his father. He took one hand while the mother held the other. He walked with the little girl into the school.

There were twelve in the nursery section. The youngest was two. Martin released the girl's hand and watched the mother take her towards the nurse. All were smiling. There was a great friendliness.

His own class was limited to ten, six of them girls. The class teacher was Miss Powell, who wore a yellow dress that reminded him of daffodils. He sat near the window and watched her face, her expressions, her gestures, trying to do well because he liked Miss Powell.

He was supposed to be lucky because he'd already learned to read and write, had progressed as far as decimals in arithmetic. He read seriously, using a dictionary to explain the meanings of new words. He read widely, especially history and foreign lands. But he liked writing best.

Almost all that he wrote was fiction. He never mentioned Tuppence, for all that he wrote Miss Powell would read and he was shy of sharing Tuppence with anyone.

He wrote as though he could still hear. His stories were all about sounds; the radio, birds, the remembered sounds of a train. When he wrote about the Battle of Hastings, there were more sounds than facts; the thrilling sounds of arrows and spears, the clashing of shields and the cries of glory.

In all ordinary subjects he advanced. But in those subjects which he had begun to learn in the past year, he was slow and unhappy.

Lip-reading was not taught as a special subject, but it was encouraged. It was part of his preparation for living among those who could hear.

He could not grasp it. He was slow and stupid. Others in his class were much quicker. He was baffled and humiliated. He thought others were laughing at his mistakes.

'Practise at home,' Miss Powell said. 'You must keep trying. Make it part of your home-work.'

Speaking was worst of all. He could not tell what his voice was doing; whether it was too high or too low. He guessed that if he became interested and excited, his voice rose to a squeak. So he tried not to become interested and excited. He spoke as little as possible, preferring to seem stupid. Sometimes he stood sulkily, defying Miss Powell to make him speak at all.

'It doesn't matter,' she said. 'I'm the only one who can hear and I don't think it's funny.'

He shook his head. He wasn't thinking of her. He was imagining the laughter of the world.

He knew she was worried about him and found pleasure in that. It was a kind of hitting back; gaining revenge for what had happened to him.

But he was taken by surprise when she produced a photograph of a pony. She showed it, then pointed to him. He knew then that his parents had told her about Tuppence.

He looked down. He wouldn't try to read the questions she was asking. He didn't believe she was truly interested. It was a trick to get him lip-reading and talking.

The next day Miss Powell surprised him again. She brought a sheepskin pad. He knew the name for it. It was a numnah.

'For your pony,' she said. 'Under the saddle.'

It wasn't new. He guessed she had used it on her own pony years ago. He knew he must accept or hurt her terribly.

'Thank you, it's very kind.'

He muttered the words, not trusting his voice. But it was a beginning.

His next short story was all about Tuppence. Soon Miss Powell knew all about the sledge and the milk churns; the ride to Grannie's store and the helicopter; the loose-box and the orchard. In these stories Tuppence was the strongest, the fastest. She could win the Grand National if she had the time.

Miss Powell asked questions about each story.

'Is it really true about the milk churns?'

'Oh yes.' Martin was surprised by her doubts. 'She got them out, day after day. All the milk was saved.'

'And is she really so strong, so fast?'

'Oh, yes.' His answer was immediate. He didn't care what his voice was doing. 'You can feel the power.'

She didn't seem to be persuading him to talk. She seemed to be doubtful that his pony could be all that he pretended.

Not until there was a tiredness in his throat did he realize that he had talked more in half an hour than he had in nearly a year.

Miss Powell asked, 'Have you hunted her yet?'

Martin shook his head. Not yet. They would go hunting for the first time on Saturday.

'Nearly the end of the season,' Miss Powell said.

Martin nodded. That was why it had to be Saturday. He hoped his mother would agree.

Preparations for hunting began on Friday evening when he brought Tuppence from the orchard.

She had roamed the orchard since the thaw, liking her freedom and always preferring grass, even poor grass, to good hay. But he brought her to the loose-box, making sure she would be dry and clean for tomorrow.

He curry-combed her thick coat, getting out the mud which had been matted by rolling. Then he brushed, making a haze of dust that tickled his nostrils and itched his hair.

'Don't brush too much,' Nathan said. 'When you brush a pony that lives out, you're taking out the natural oil. She needs that oil to keep her warm in wind and rain.'

Martin was careful about her legs. Nathan always said, no legs, no pony, and the phrase was in Martin's mind as he brushed. He went to one knee, making sure that the brush did not bump the chestnut on the inside of each leg.

The chestnuts were hard lumps which looked

dead. But they were not. Break one of them and a pony might bleed to death.

He took a soft brush to the gentle places inside her back legs. This was the stifle, corresponding to a boy's knee. The flesh here was very tender.

Martin remembered what Nathan had told him; this was where to look if you suspected cruelty to a circus horse. The long whip of the trainer flicked the tender stifle, leaving no marks on the satin coat for the public to see.

Her mane was unruly. It would not lie one side or the other. It fuzzed up like a gorse bush. Her tail was long and expressive. She used it to express her moods. One swish meant surprise. A quick swish meant impatience. A looping movement meant she'd had enough.

Martin used the soft brush for her head. She fidgeted as he got out the mud around her ears. She screwed up her eyes as he brushed her wide forehead.

He realized that in many ways she was like him. He wriggled when his mother scrubbed behind his ears. He had always hated having his eyes done in the bath.

The business with comb and brush convinced Tuppence that something was brewing. She looked around, full of questions, impatient for whatever it was, especially if it was food.

Martin crouched to her feet. She gave up each foot reluctantly, impatient of being on three legs.

The hoof pick took out the mud, tracing the shape of the frog. Martin was careful not to touch the frog. It was triangular in shape, made of elastic horn. It took the concussion of each step.

Nathan had shown him diagrams of the skeleton of a horse's foot. It was wonderfully complex, all bones and cartilages and ligaments. Its outer casing was of horn, corresponding to the claws of other animals. Inside were the sensitive tissues and fibres. If you could see them, they would be soft and red and would bleed easily.

Martin was fascinated that a hoof could be so complicated. Nathan had compared its three parts with the boot, the sock and the foot of a man.

He gave Tuppence hay and water and settled her for the night. Then he began the chore of cleaning saddle and bridle. First a wet sponge on the leather, then saddle soap, as yellow as floor polish. It was a slow business. He was bored. He wanted to skip underneath the saddle flaps, but Nathan was watching.

'It's not only the shine,' Nathan said. 'Soaping strengthens the leather. Leather isn't strong when it's dry. It breaks easy.'

He made Martin spend a long time on bridle and reins, for a dry rein would be brittle and a snapping rein would be disastrous.

'Mustn't take any chances,' Nathan said. 'Your mother's worried as it is.'

Martin knew how worried his mother was. She would not have agreed if Jane hadn't promised to look after him.

Martin sighed. Fancy having a girl looking after you. He was astonished that his mother could make such conditions. Surely she realized he was quite capable of looking after himself?

'You better put up with it,' Nathan said. 'You won't be going at all else.'

Martin thought about Jane as he rubbed in the saddle soap. Better make a good job of it or Jane would notice and go all superior. Typical girl, Martin thought.

It wasn't fair, of course. Jane was experienced and efficient. She'd never pass the eleven-plus, but she could ride anything on four legs. She'd been in the saddle before she could walk.

But Martin resented the condition which his mother had made. He made up his mind to show Jane what he and his Tuppence could do.

In the morning he was in the yard half an hour early, waiting for Jane to come across the moor. She rode a neat chestnut, three-parts clipped and fit and sharp. It wasn't a moorland pony. Her father had bought it cheaply and Jane was schooling it for hunter trials. If it won awards, Harvey would sell at a handsome profit and buy another. Then the process of schooling would begin all over again. Jane seldom rode a pony for longer than six months.

'Nice pony,' Nathan said.

Martin pulled a face. Not as good as Tuppence. All looks and show-off. He was violently prejudiced against the chestnut on sight. He was afraid it would prove much faster than Tuppence.

'Hullo,' Jane said, reaching the gate. 'You ready? It's a long way.'

Mr. and Mrs. Manningham had heard her

coming. They came from the house, one proud, the other worried. They talked with Jane while Martin went to the box.

Tuppence had heard the other pony. She was as excited as Robinson Crusoe when he found another footprint. It seemed that for months she'd been living on a desert island, without chance to hob-nob with one of her kind.

She came bustling out of the box, hurrying to the gate and stretching her neck towards the chestnut. Her expression was earnest. Her top lip trembled. She wanted to be liked.

The chestnut touched noses briefly, then flinched, rejecting the overtures of this moorland tramp. It looked down its nose and turned away with a pained expression.

Tuppence still reached above the gate, sure they could be friends. Martin saw the in-and-out of her nostrils. He knew she was nickering, begging the chestnut to stay for a natter.

Jane laughed, looking down. There seemed to be derision in the laughter, mocking Tuppence for being a moorland tramp.

Martin was stung. All right, he thought, clambering from gate to saddle. You'll soon find out.

Mrs. Manningham drew near. For a dreadful moment he thought she was going to ask about his vest. But she only said, 'Are you warm enough?'

He nodded, begging her not to fuss. His father reached up, giving him the half-crowns for the 'cap'.

'We'll be there,' Mr. Manningham said. 'We'll drive over in time for the meet.'

Jane's chestnut was fretting. It led the way down the hill and across the bridge. It arched its neck and displayed its tail, refusing to wait for Tuppence.

Tuppence trotted earnestly, trying to catch up. She couldn't believe the elegant chestnut didn't want to talk.

They crossed the moor to the highway and the hazard of cars. Most drivers were sympathetic, understanding that the ponies were excited and that to alarm them would risk a fall and broken knees. But some roared by with defiant exhausts, as though they alone had a right to the road. Then Jane hurled abuse.

Martin grinned. He couldn't hear what she was saying, but he remembered her special language.

Lorry-drivers were the most considerate. Motor-cyclists were the least. In three quarters of an hour of slipping and sliding, Martin learned to admire lorry-drivers and to hate motor-cyclists as though they were goggled devils.

'Clown,' Jane shouted. 'Idiot. Nit.'

The last meet of the season was held traditionally at Peat House Inn, on a high shoulder of the moor.

The inn got its name from the peat fires which had burned in its big hearth. The peat had been cut in July, left to dry, then brought in by pack-pony to give a long, slow heat.

It had been cheap, since it could be cut for nothing on the moor, but women had hated its dust.

Now the peat-fire was only a memory. The inn burned logs for convenience.

Cars were thick around the inn. They had made

long journeys from towns and city, for many who had never ridden and had never seen a fox, liked the hounds, the horses, the colourful coats of the hunt servants. Some carried their interest beyond the meet and followed on foot. One tireless enthusiast liked to do it by bicycle.

Martin saw his parents' car as he trotted up the hill. They were watching. He guessed his mother had imagined an accident for every mile.

Tuppence responded to the sounds of hounds, the sight of other ponies. She'd given up trying to convince the chestnut that they had plenty to talk about. She felt sure that among so many others, there must be one who wouldn't say no.

Martin laughed at her enthusiasm, but underneath the laughter was a kind of sadness. Tuppence had been born on the moor, and moorland ponies moved in groups. Their herd instinct was still strong. Tuppence hadn't forgotten it. Half the excitement of a meet was being among other ponies.

Martin watched Jane. She was talking with other young riders. They were laughing. He wondered what they were laughing at; if they were laughing at him.

For a moment he was sure they were laughing at him, and his resentment hardened to hatred. Then he felt a touch on his knee and saw his father.

His father was saying something. Martin couldn't see the words but he knew it was encouragement. He held Tuppence on a tight rein as the hounds came around in inquiry.

The hounds had brave names; Bullet, Cromwell,

Jason, Emperor. They were strong and lean and sharp with hunger. They had not eaten since the day before yesterday.

Martin watched the huntsman. He was speaking to the hounds, recognizing each instantly although their brown heads and black patches on white bodies seemed identical. On Thursday he had hunted the bitch pack. Today he had the dogs.

The whipper-in trailed his whip. One of the more reluctant hounds took the hint and joined the pack around the huntsman's horse.

Martin noticed how calm and patient the hunt horses were. They were professionals, making amateurs of the excited ponies.

The hunt provided huntsman and whipper-in with big horses, in their prime at seven years old. They had been imported from Ireland, fully grown and developed, strong of bone and big of spirit. After three seasons hunting the steep moorland, they would be sold to other hunts where the country was flat and the demands were less.

The landlord of the inn brought out the stirrup cup. There was sherry, port and whisky for adults, orangeade for the children. Martin took the glass of orangeade. He didn't want it, but it was one of the old courtesies.

He noticed how important these old courtesies were. Men lifted their hats to women. Each boy touched his cap to the master. None drank until the master raised his glass.

It seemed a world away from impatient drivers and leather-jackets and grab all you can get.

A hunt supporter came around with the cap.

Each member contributed to hunt expenses in addition to the annual subscription. The cap for adults was £1. For juniors it was five shillings. But some gave more because hunt expenses were high. A good horse cost £300. A hound cost £50, sometimes more.

Only farmers did not have to pay. They hunted for nothing because the future of hunting depended on the co-operation of farmers.

Years ago it had been different. A farmer had been compelled to allow the hunt on his acres. It had been part of his agreement with the landlord. But big estates had broken up. Many farmers now owned the land they farmed. They could refuse entry if they wished.

So the hunt tried to keep and deserve the support of farmers. If hedges or gates were broken, if crops were destroyed, the hunt paid compensation or supporters volunteered to do the repairs.

Martin looked around, surprised by the enthusiasm of these supporters; wondering what the hunt achieved to justify so much time, so much money. Thousands of pounds every year. He wondered where the money came from, then found an answer.

The point-to-point meeting, held each spring, was the most popular means of raising money. Entry to those who walked was free, although you were expected to pay half-a-crown for a race-card. Cars paid £1. The more cars, the more money. But the more rain, the more mud, and mud kept away the cars.

Martin liked point-to-point meetings. He had

gone often with his father. Many of the horses were owned by families he knew or had heard about. Some of the riders were elder brothers of boys he had known before his accident.

Prizes were small, seldom more than £20 for the winner, but racing was keen because of local competition. Years ago his father had dreamed aloud of owning a point-to-point horse with Martin riding it. Now this dream was forgotten. But Jane would ride over fences when she was old enough.

Harvey made no secret of his intention to buy a good horse for Jane to ride in ladies' races. Martin thought she'd either win or break her neck.

The huntsman whined his horn, telling the hounds that social courtesies were over. The day's work was about to begin.

It was then that two vans came over the hill. They were travelling fast. They slowed as they reached the inn, then pulled up a hundred yards away.

The back doors opened. Youths and girls in duffel coats jumped out. Martin was bewildered. He didn't understand when Jane cried, 'It's the anti's.'

Two girls carried a banner. They unrolled it and held up poles. 'BAN ALL HUNTING' the banner said.

Excitement was immediate. The huntsman and whipper-in snapped their whips, keeping their hounds close. Horses and ponies fretted. Supporters on foot waved their sticks.

Martin had read about the demonstrators. They wanted publicity for their campaign to ban all hunting by Government decree. They had made progress. People in towns and cities were expressing disgust of all blood sports. Many were distressed and amazed that the R.S.P.C.A. supported hunting as preferable to shooting, poisoning and trapping. There had been quarrels within the R.S.P.C.A.

He saw that most of the demonstrators were young, many of them less than twenty. There were more girls than youths, but the youths seemed to be the leaders.

Two ran behind a wall, bending low to screen what they were carrying. They opened a sack and threw out meat. They knew the hounds were hungry. They knew a well-filled hound would not want to hunt.

One yielded to temptation. It ran towards the meat. Martin saw the angry shape as the whipper-in cracked his whip. The hound sank low and crept back apologetically.

Spectators ran to gather the meat. Martin saw that his father was among them. He was surprised, for his father wasn't an ardent supporter. Mr. Manningham allowed the hunt to cross his land, but he had grumbled often. Now he was running with the determination of an ardent supporter. A dark-haired youth plucked his sleeve, trying to stop him. Mr. Manningham lashed with his fist. His face was furious

Other men were struggling. The landlord was protesting. A spectacled youth jumped at the master's horse, trying to drag him down. The master used his hunting crop, and the youth fell back.

Martin was ashamed. He thought the scuffling was pitiful and silly. Then something happened to make him a part of it.

Two girls were standing on a wall. They were throwing. The sudden terror of the horses told him what they were throwing.

He looked down and saw one near Tuppence. He slid from the saddle, still holding the reins. He stamped on the firework as it fizzed.

Now Tuppence was wheeling so fast he could not hold her. He looked for his father. Mr. Manningham appeared, meat in either hand. He threw the meat to the back of his car and took the bridle, sitting down to her strength as she reared.

Martin ran to help Jane. Her chestnut was down, its leg tangled with reins. He held the leg while she eased away the rein. The chestnut lurched up. Both leaned their strengths into it, holding its fright. They looked towards the vans.

The demonstrators were running. The girls were laughing. They leaped into the vans. Doors slammed. Engines roared. They were away. The 'raid' had taken less than five minutes, although to Martin it had seemed much longer.

Hunt supporters watched them go. Now they were more excited than angry. They boasted about what they had done to the fellow with spectacles. Jane claimed to have kicked one. Mrs. Manningham asked what the police were doing, allowing it to happen.

Martin wasn't interested in who had won the scuffle. He was shocked that those who pretended to be concerned about wild animals could throw fireworks among horses and ponies.

'City louts,' his father said. 'Looking for a spree.'

Martin saw that the scuffle had achieved nothing. Except to make small people of all who had taken part.

# CHAPTER SIX

THE horn whined and hounds moved. Martin touched his cap to his parents. Mrs. Manningham called something and Jane answered.

The huntsman led the hounds, his whip extended to keep them back. The whipper-in followed. Then came the master and his wife. Theirs were positions of privilege, several yards ahead of other adults.

The juniors were last. Jane pulled a face, nodding towards a woman on a grey horse. She was notorious. She was convinced that children were nuisances who needed to be taught good manners.

All the young were polite to her face and rude as soon as her back was turned. None took any notice of her as soon as the hounds were running.

'Boy,' the woman cried. 'Get that pony back.'

Martin didn't hear the words but he saw the expression, livid with indignation. He checked Tuppence, looking down, feeling a great hatred swell like a balloon. The woman personified the old arrogance which made anyone on a big horse superior to everyone in the world.

'Take no notice,' Jane said. 'We'll lose her as soon as they begin to gallop.'

Hounds turned from the road to the heather and

bracken. They crossed the moor towards a copse where foxes had been reported.

Yesterday volunteers had stopped the earths, preventing any fox from finding easy refuge below ground. The huntsman took the hounds in, chivvying them with high cries like the cries of a night bird. There was a trampling of bracken, a cracking of whips. The hounds were busy.

The master glanced around the riders, making sure that discipline was good. Senior members were posted at the four corners of the wood, ready to cry if the fox broke. Others gathered in social groups, talking about point-to-point horses.

The young riders made their own group, but again Martin was an outsider. He had known many of the boys years ago, had played football and cricket with them. But he was different now. Their embarrassment made him feel different.

He kept a little apart, talking to Tuppence in a low voice, running his hand down her neck. His deafness made it seem that his only friend was the pony.

A fox broke on the north side. The observer let out a wild yell. The huntsman echoed it. The first hound to get on the scent was Bullet, always the wisest and most determined. The sound Bullet made had the horses dancing.

Jane flashed a glance and let her chestnut go. It thundered up the rise. Martin sent Tuppence in pursuit, pushing her, begging her to show the chestnut what she could do.

Over the ridge they went, then down the other side. Galloping downhill was frightening. He dug in his knees and screwed up his eyes from the wind. He tried to shorten the reins into a double handful, but Tuppence wasn't having any. She passed two ponies, another, then another. She passed a big hunter, then the grey horse.

Martin did not dare glance to see what the woman thought of being passed by a little Dartmoor. He leaned forward, excited by his pony's generosity, feeling her hammer at the hill on the other side.

Jane stood in the stirrups, giving her chestnut a breather. She laughed, her cheeks burned by the wind. There was no derision now in the laughter. She was pleased to win the unofficial race. But at the same time she was congratulating him on making it a race worth winning.

Martin wasn't downcast by losing. Tuppence had shown her willingness. He suspected that she might have caught the chestnut had he not tried to stop her coming down the hill.

Half an hour later they had another long gallop, another excuse for a race. Again Jane stole a length or two at the start, flinging back a glance, defying him to catch her.

He understood the challenge. So did Tuppence. She put down her head and began a pounding gallop. Her seriousness made the race important. It seeemed she'd had enough of the chestnut's airs and graces. She was out to take it down a peg or two.

They came to a stream. He did not realize there was a stream until the chestnut jumped. In a second of alarm he realized that he had never asked Tuppence to jump. Perhaps she would check or stumble, dumping him up to his neck. There was no time to consider. He trusted her and her stride did not falter.

She jumped the stream and pounded again. Martin's reward was Jane's surprise as they came alongside. She was flushed and breathless. She forced her chestnut, trying to shake off the little Dartmoor.

But Tuppence clung. Her determination made it plain that she had no intention of giving in.

Jane stood in the stirrups, drawing in her pony. The chestnut stopped gladly. The little Dartmoor went pounding on, slowing only when she was sure that the chestnut had given in.

'Too fast,' Jane said.

Martin knew that. He hadn't the breath to explain that it hadn't been his idea.

Hounds checked for a long time. They were cast in a wide arc, their noses down, their tails waving. The official name for their tails was 'sterns'. It was as much an offence to call a tail a tail as it was to call the red jackets red. Hunting pink was the name for the red jackets. It didn't make sense until you realized that 'pink' wasn't a description of the colour. It was the name of a famous tailor who had made hunting coats.

Such lore was part of hunting, but Martin didn't attach much importance to it. He thought that a huntsman's coat was no less red because there had been a tailor called Pink. But Jane gave all the lore the importance of a religion.

She would no more refer to a fox's paw than she

would shout in church. The paw was a pad. The face was a mask. The tail was a brush.

She had nicknames for the fox. Sometimes it was 'Charlie' in memory of Charles James Fox, a politician who had died in 1806. Sometimes it was 'Frenchie' because the fox on the southern part of Dartmoor was smaller, redder and sharper than in other parts. A Frenchman was supposed to be small and sharp and clever.

Hounds picked up the scent again, but the fox had gained time by doubling, then redoubling. The scent led to a plantation of spruce, and everyone knew the pack would never get Charlie out of that.

Martin imagined the fox safe somewhere and smiling. He wasn't sorry. He was glad that hunting was no organized slaughter with success guaranteed.

His hands were stiff with cold. He groped in a top pocket for chocolate, breaking it and holding out a half to Jane. They ate fruit and nut, and waited a long time before the huntsman admitted that the fox had won.

Hounds moved to another copse. Another wait in the freezing wind, then sudden excitement and shrill cries. Again hounds were streaming across the heather. They looked good, a ripple of colour in the bleak wilderness. Martin's blood responded. He was warmed by the sight. He understood why hunting had claimed the enthusiasm of generations.

This time Jane waited for him, not making a race of it. He could see her remembering her promise to his mother. His resentment came back. He waved a hand, telling her to go on. But she kept the chestnut beside him, making herself his guardian.

There was sudden hostility between them. He thought all the world must see the girl looking after him.

They trotted miserably, neither speaking nor looking. Now they were not two members of a hunt. They were isolated by their private war.

Jane gave up. She let her chestnut go, resolved to enjoy the rest of the day. Martin followed, keeping away from her, refusing to let Tuppence carry on the rivalry.

Hounds killed a dog fox. It was heavy with wool, proof that it had recently killed a lamb.

Martin understood that a dog fox plundered in spring not only because it was hungry but because it killed for the vixen. When the cubs were born, the father would look after them, too. The fox was one of the most faithful fathers among wild animals.

Momentarily he thought of the vixen, waiting somewhere for its mate. Then he watched the hounds tear the fox to shreds. He saw the huntsman's horn and imagined its long, steady cry, signalling the kill.

In a way he was relieved. The kill meant the day was over. Presumably they could go home now. He was frozen. His feet were dead. He could not straighten his fingers. But the master decided otherwise. It was too early to go home. The season was almost over. They could not waste the last hours.

Hounds moved towards trees. Jane went with

them, not glancing back. Tuppence would have followed, but Martin had had enough. Tuppence didn't want to break from the others. It seemed like quitting. She moved sluggishly. She sulked. Her walk became slower and slower.

Martin began to regret the impulse to break away. He had no watch, no means except the sky of guessing the time. Clouds shut out what passed for the sun, but he guessed it to be nearer four than three. He hunched his shoulders, trying to protect his ears from the wind. He thought of log flames and steaming stew and the blessed warmth of being home. He couldn't believe that he would ever be warm again.

Jane asked other young riders. No, they hadn't seen him. What did it matter?

Jane snapped, 'Of course it matters.'

She was angry with herself for not fulfilling her promise to his mother. She let the silence remind them of Martin's deafness. The boys thought about it.

One said, 'He'll be all right.'

Jane supposed so. But she stood in the stirrups, scanning the skyline, hoping to see Martin coming back.

They hunted another hour. Jane glanced at her watch. Half past four. The master would turn for home now. Hounds were tired. So were the horses.

Master and hounds turned towards Hodden Cross, where the hound-van and the horse-boxes were waiting. Jane rode with a group of girls and boys to the highway. There she turned one way, while they turned the other.

Jane hacked towards the big hill which had Shepherds Hill and her father's farm on the other side. She watched the wilderness on either side, still hoping for a sign of Martin. The hills were shut in by mist. Cold rain pecked at her eyelids.

A grass track ran beside the road. She turned her chestnut to it, saving its feet from tarmac. Cars hurried by. Now they were not hostile. She was too tired to shout abuse to roaring exhausts. The cars were welcome. They were a link with the twentieth century. On either side the wild moor could have been a hundred years ago.

Jane buttoned her collar to her chin. She tried to tell herself that Martin was already home. He'd taken a short cut and was already warm and eating a hot meal. But she knew it wasn't true.

She came to the cross-roads and Grannie's store. On a sudden hope she got down and opened the door, asking Grannie if she'd seen Martin.

'Why?' Grannie spoke sharply, sniffing for news. 'What's happened?'

Jane didn't answer. She was already scrambling to the saddle. Behind her Grannie said, 'He should never have gone hunting. His mother should never have let him.'

Jane guessed what would happen. Grannie would tell the next customer that something had happened, hinting criticism of the mother; and the next customer would ask how she knew and Grannie would answer, 'Jane Harvey told me.' So it would be passed on and on until it got back to Mrs.

Manningham who'd blame Jane for telling Grannie about it in the first place.

That was the sort of mischief Grannie could do. Jane groaned, looking ahead to trouble.

She turned towards Shepherds Hill. From the ridge she saw the farm-buildings, the farm-house and Nathan's cottage. The scene was peaceful. It didn't know that bad news was coming down the hill.

'Where is he?' Mrs. Manningham cried.

Jane slipped from the saddle, resting her tired pony. She fumbled what she had decided to say, feeling her guilt.

'I trusted you.' Mrs. Manningham's eyes were wide. 'I would never have let him. . . .'

Farmer Manningham put a hand on her arm. Blaming Jane was no use.

He asked, 'Where did you last see him?'

Jane tried to remember. 'Near Ledger Rock. They'd just killed and the master took hounds on to Curlew Copse. But Martin didn't follow and when I looked round, I couldn't see him.'

It sounded weak and careless. She tried to put it right by adding, 'I thought he'd gone home. It was terribly cold and I thought. . . .'

'Ledger Rock then,' Mr. Manningham said. 'We can get near by car, then walk from there.'

They knew Martin would not still be at Ledger Rock, but they had to start somewhere. The moor covered two hundred square miles. He might be anywhere.

'You go home, Jane. Your pony's tired.'

Jane began to protest, wanting to make amends. Then she admitted it was good sense. She walked her pony away, not glancing back to Mrs. Manningham, not wanting to see the accusation.

'We'll find him.' The farmer grinned to reassure his wife. 'Probably we'll meet him on the way home.'

He hurried to his car. Mrs. Manningham got in the other side. Nathan opened the gate and the car sped.

Martin felt the difference. This part of the moor was as dark as evil. Its cold had a special shiver.

There was no sign of bracken or heather. There were no granite boulders, patterned with lichen. Nothing except this dark silence.

Then he realized. He recognized it. He'd seen it as a sinister patch on a map. He'd heard about it when he was small and fascinated by stories of the moor.

He had wandered into Crockin Bog.

All his life he'd heard tales of its dangers. Blunder into it and you were doomed. The more you struggled, the deeper you went, down and down like the drowning. Travellers had been lost in Crockin Bog.

He looked up, hoping for help, for someone, anyone. The creep down of rain was menacing. He could not see the hills. Five minutes ago the hills had been there. Now they were shut out. The mist of rain was drifting down. He felt it soaking his shoulders, misting his eyelids, crying down his cheeks like tears.

He realized he was alone ... and in danger.

Mr. Manningham drove into the rain. He knew what his wife was thinking; it had been folly to let the boy go.

After a while she said, 'You wanted him to be like other boys. You wouldn't admit that since the accident, that now he can never be like other boys.'

He made a reassuring sound. He tried to sound more confident than he felt.

'All day I've been worrying,' Mrs. Manningham said. 'It's not fair, not fair to me. I know you say I molly-coddle him, but trying to make him like other boys, that's not fair to me.'

He repeated the reassuring sound. He knew it wasn't fair. Yet molly-coddling would not be fair to the boy.

He said, 'He'll be all right.'

Then he put his foot down. There was little traffic. The season was too early for tourist cars and coaches. Usually his wife glanced a warning if he drove fast, but she did not glance now.

Martin remembered something. He remembered Nathan saying that wild animals did not go down in bogs. They knew the unmarked paths. They were guided by instinct.

Then he remembered something else. Tuppence was a moorland pony. She had been bred to survive the hazards of the moor.

He told Tuppence what she must do. He slapped her neck and dropped the reins. She didn't move. She stretched her neck, stiff with suspicion.

He waited what seemed a long time, but Tuppence would not move.

'Not Jane's fault,' Mr. Manningham said. 'The boy didn't like a girl looking after him.' He fidgeted behind a slow car, looking for an opportunity to pass. 'Not surprising,' he added, finding the opportunity and sending his car leaping forward. 'I wouldn't have liked it at his age.'

Mrs. Manningham's glance was sharp. 'You were different. You could hear.'

'But being deaf, that doesn't make him a cissy. You've got to look at it from the boy's point of view.'

She didn't answer. She thought it very silly.

They reached the nearest point to Ledger Rock. Misted rain was creeping down, almost obscuring it. They got out, looking up to the rock, feeling the immensity of the moor.

'He's somewhere,' Mrs. Manningham said. 'Trying to find his way home.'

She felt her own helplessness. She wished that this hour could be over in a flash; that it could be an hour's time with Martin safely found.

The ridge from Ledger Rock fell steeply, then climbed again; and on the other side of the second ridge was ... Mr. Manningham daren't think of it. He stopped himself saying what waited on the other side of the ridge.

Mrs. Manningham didn't guess. She knew about the bog, she'd heard tales about it when she was a child. But she didn't know precisely where it was.

His hand tightened on her arm, asking her to

hurry. It was a long climb, but he made her hurry. If the boy had blundered into Crockin Bog . . . .

Martin waited as long as he could. He dared not touch her with his heels, dared not urge her in any direction. Only she knew where it was safe to step.

Then he guessed. She was waiting for him to get off, to make her free.

He slipped his feet from the stirrups, looking down, mistrusting the ground on either side. He got off backwards, slipping over her rump. Now he had no control. She was free.

In a flash of panic he imagined her trotting the invisible paths, too quickly for him to follow. But Tuppence moved slowly, thinking about each step, her nose almost touching the ground. Each step left a hoof-print, and he stepped in it.

Their movement was as slow as a funeral. The path was not straight. It meandered.

Tuppence stopped for long minutes, considering each turn. Then he stopped also, touching her tail but not speaking. He knew what one false step could do.

Mrs. Manningham guessed why her husband was hurrying, dragging her up the slope to the ridge. She guessed what was on the other side.

'He'll keep still,' Mr. Manningham said. 'He'll know how dangerous it is.'

Both of them saw the truth in that instant. If it was not safe for Martin to move, it would not be possible for them to reach him. They would be able only to stand and watch.

Mrs. Manningham made a sobbing sound.

They reached the ridge and looked down. The bog was oval in shape, with a hill at each end and a long ridge on each side. A hundred years ago Dartmoor people had called it the Devil's Basin.

For a long while they could see no movement. Their eyes were blurred by rain. They crept nearer and suddenly they saw him. They thought he was standing still. Then they realized. He was moving behind the pony.

She made a warning sound, but the farmer's grip on her hand tightened. They couldn't help. Any sound might frighten the pony.

'Do you think he sees us?' Mrs. Manningham asked.

He hoped not. If the boy looked up, anything might happen.

Twilight thickened, but now their eyes were accustomed. They could see the black movement of the pony.

'She's not going straight,' Mrs. Manningham said.

He didn't answer. Old moormen had always said the paths wandered. He was thanking his luck that he had bought a Dartmoor pony. Only the local breed would have found the path.

Boy and pony were going away from them, towards the opposite ridge. They stayed until the danger was almost over. Then they went up the slope towards the car.

They hurried, half running, half stumbling. The farmer snatched open a door, helping in his wife.

then he ran to the other door, feeling mud thicken on his boots.

The engine spluttered. He swore at it. Its sudden straining roar could have been a tiger breaking from a cage.

He felt the wheels struggling in grass which had become mud. In a moment of panic he didn't think they were going to do it. Then the car lurched. It was free. It was gathering speed.

He drove in an arc to the other side of the valley. He turned off the road, getting the car as near the ridge as he dared. Then the hurry of climbing began again.

'You stay – you're tired out.'

Mrs. Manningham didn't even answer. She struggled to keep pace with him.

They reached the ridge and looked down. Boy and pony were near the edge of the bog. So nearly there that suddenly they were too afraid to move.

Again she wanted to cry out. Again her husband gripped her arm. They waited tensely.

Then Tuppence decided. Four quick steps and she was out. The boy was safe. They saw him put his arms around the pony, hiding his face, hiding the tears of relief and pride.

His father reached him first, coming so suddenly that Tuppence jumped. Mr. Manningham made reassuring noises. Her first thought was that he was Satan, arising suddenly out of the ground. Her second was that he had something in his pocket. She nuzzled for whatever it was, and Mr. Manningham was angry because he had nothing.

Martin turned towards his mother. She was

laughing and crying, her hands feeling the rain in his shoulders.

They moved from the bog and its evil silence. Martin took his mother's hand, persuading her fingers to clutch the pony's mane. She laughed, surprised by the help which Tuppence gave.

They climbed to the ridge, then went down the other side. They reached the car. Its headlights were as bright as dragon's eyes.

Mr. and Mrs. Manningham got in while Martin struggled up on Tuppence. The car crept, keeping pace with the pony.

The mother watched the boy's tiredness, telling herself that as soon as they reached Shepherds Hill there would be a hot bath, a hot meal and the big blaze of the fire.

The father watched the pony, chuckling because the pony had more sense than he'd believed.

They reached Grannie's store. Mrs. Manningham remembered that Martin had eaten only fruit and nut since breakfast. More chocolate would be better than nothing. She ducked out and bought two bars.

'Found your boy then?' Grannie asked.

Mrs. Manningham was surprised, wondering how Grannie knew. Then she said, 'Yes, we're on the way home,' making nothing of it, spoiling Grannie's story.

'Bound to happen,' Grannie said. 'Wilful little pony like that.'

Mrs. Manningham answered before she realized.

'Not wilful. Tuppence is a wonderful little pony.'

Then she saw the joke. Two hours ago she had condemned Tuppence in stronger words than that.

She gave the chocolate to Martin and ducked back to the car. She thought they would move at once, but her husband pointed, waiting for the boy.

Martin broke a piece of chocolate. Tuppence heard the crackle of paper and looked back to nudge his boot. He leaned to give her the piece. He broke the bar again, and again she heard and nudged. She had all the bar in this way while his mother complained of the waste.

'It never is,' Mr. Manningham said. 'They're partners. They share.'

Tuppence still nudged when the bar was gone. She wouldn't believe it until he showed her the blue paper and tinfoil. Then she made do with the blue paper, spitting out the tinfoil.

Martin didn't mention the second bar. He broke that furtively as they continued towards Shepherds Hill. They saw the light of Nathan's cottage while they were still two miles away.

Nathan was warned by the headlights. He was waiting at the opened gate. He held up a lantern and Tuppence stopped abruptly, contemplating the light, suspecting goblins.

Martin laughed. The heroine of the bog was now pretending to be a coward. He called through the darkness, asking Nathan to speak. Tuppence recognized the voice and hurried up the hill.

Martin got down. He didn't need to lead her to the box. He dropped the reins to her wither and she knew the way. Nathan had the door open and she went in to warm mash. She looked up once. Her nose was freckled with it.

Mrs. Manningham hurried to the kitchen, throwing more logs on the fire, then laying the table for the meal which should have been tea and had become supper.

She called from the porch, 'Come and get those wet clothes off. You'll catch your death.'

Martin knew she was there but didn't answer. He stayed with Tuppence, telling Nathan what had happened. Nathan nodded appreciatively, not believing half of it. He knew how boys exaggerated. They watched Tuppence reach the last of the mash. She ate greedily, dirtily, smudging her nose with the brown stuff. Then she looked out of the box towards the orchard.

'She wants to go,' Nathan said.

Martin took her to the orchard. She dropped her nose to the mud inside the gate. She got down on her knees and rolled, over, then back, then over again, rolling the mud into her sweat. She stood up and shook herself. Then she cropped thin grass.

It seemed small reward for her hard day. Martin compared it with the fussing, the drying with hay and straw, which other ponies received. He wanted to give her what others gave their ponies, but Nathan assured him that a moorland pony asked only to roll, then to be left to its grass.

'I'd give you anything,' Martin said. 'And this is all you want.'

Meanwhile his father was phoning Jane, telling her what had happened.

'The pony got him out,' Mr. Manningham shouted. 'Never put a foot wrong coming through the bog.'

He was in a good humour, laughing as though the whole episode had been a fine joke. His wife couldn't understand it. She didn't realize it was the laughter of deep relief.

# CHAPTER SEVEN

JANE came more often. She rode the chestnut over almost every day, showing that in her way she was as lonely as Martin had been.

Shepherds Hill had never really liked her. Mrs Manningham had mistrusted her skill with horses, more like a boy than a girl and capable of such language. Even Nathan had turned a cold shoulder, blaming her for what Harvey did to the ponies.

Only Mr. Manningham had given her the benefit of any number of doubts. Not her fault, he used to say. She'd been taught all her life that ponies were something you bought and sold, like soap. They didn't have personalities. They didn't want to belong. They did what you wanted or else ... He didn't blame Jane for her attitude to ponies. He guessed she'd never been given a chance.

Now she kept coming, looking for a welcome, grateful when Mrs. Manningham invited her to supper on schooldays or to dinner on Saturdays. She seemed fascinated by Martin's relationship with Tuppence. It wasn't the relationship of animal and owner, the one to do what the other wanted. It was the relationship of friends who had shared adventures.

Jane had ridden fifty or more ponies in her ten

years. As soon as she got one traffic safe and fit, her father found a buyer and she was teaching another. Her experience was much wider than Martin's would ever be, but she had never shared a relationship as deep and good-humoured as this.

She envied it. She liked to watch. She began to see that she had missed something important.

A year ago she had ridden Tuppence and the little filly had been an idiot, all moods and tremble, afraid of everything new, so frightened of her father that Harvey had never been able to catch her. They had despaired of ever finding a buyer. After periods of trial she had always come back like a bad penny. That's why they had kept the price down when Mr. Manningham had mentioned a pony for Martin. They had been half afraid that she'd be back again within days.

Jane had thought her the most stupid pony she had ever ridden. Show her the stick and she became as stupid as a dunce. Drive her into a fence of poles and she did everything wrong. Teach her good manners in traffic and she passed a timber lorry without flinching, then refused to pass a flapping tarpaulin.

Jane had been as astonished as her father when the Manninghams had not sent the pony back. At the back of her mind had been a feeling of guilt, wondering what might happen to Martin when the pony shied or bucked or jibbed.

Now there was no stupidity. Martin didn't have to catch her. His footsteps were enough. She came to the gate of the orchard, nuckering in a where've-you-been way. He didn't have to tip-toe to get the bit in and the bridle on. She held her head down, almost doing it for him. Then, when they rode across the moor, he didn't have to kick her or show the stick. She was willing. She shirked nothing. She jumped streams and gullies as though she liked showing off.

Jane saw that she enjoyed being ridden. She was indignant if he did not take her wherever he wanted to go.

At first she tried to mock the relationship as sentimental. A pony needed to know who was boss. A few smacks did no harm. But the mockery wouldn't work.

Tuppence could do all that the proud chestnut could do and sometimes a little more. Jane gave up challenging Martin to races across the heather. She liked winning and the chestnut was not sure to win, even when she stole a length or two at the start. She was humiliated when the little mongrel kept pace with the chestnut, then drew ahead and there was nothing she could do about it.

Gradually she realized that Martin had more than she had. Tuppence was his and would never be sold. Tuppence trusted him and he trusted her, and both responded to this sense of security.

Gradually Jane began to wish for a pony of her own; one which would always be hers and would not be sold as soon as it was fit and schooled and worth more than her father had given. It didn't have to be an expensive pony. One of the moorland mongrels would do, provided its legs were sound and its spirit was generous, provided it had a personality to make it different from any other in the world.

She dreamed about having her own; as fiercely hers as Tuppence was fiercely Martin's. But she knew it wouldn't work. If she did have such a pony and learned to love it, her father couldn't be trusted. He would see the possibility of a quick profit and would look for a buyer, then sell it secretly while she was at school. She sighed, knowing her father wouldn't understand. You couldn't be sentimental about ponies when they were your livelihood. You didn't give them names. You gave them values. The pony worth £60 was three times as important as one worth £20, no matter what its personality or how your heart was touched.

She tried to tell Martin a little of what she was thinking, leaving out only her suspicions of her father. She didn't know how much he understood. But she knew they were better friends than before and that was something.

Martin understood more than she supposed. He couldn't read her words, but he was learning to read expressions. He watched as she scratched Tuppence's neck in an absent-minded way. He felt her sadness, her loneliness. She shook it off at once, but he saw it in glimpses and tried to understand.

While their friendship was developing, something was happening between their ponies.

On the day of the hunt Jane's chestnut had been superior, looking down its nose. Tuppence at first had looked for a cosy natter. When that had been spurned, she had taken umbrage and made the chestnut a rival.

Now all that was changed. The chestnut admitted its mistake. It begged forgiveness. It followed Tuppence when they grazed, grazing where she chose, moving when she moved. It let Tuppence have first grab when carrots were being offered.

The transformation was comical, Jane and Martin laughed, amused by the filly's swank as much as by the chestnut's deference. Tuppence was a good actress. She could be coy, bashful, bold, sullen, gay.

Now Tuppence had to be first. First through the gate, first down the hill; first to drink from the moorland streams. The chestnut apologized when it forgot its place and found itself in front.

Bay filly and chestnut gelding saw plenty of each other during those evenings in May and those long Saturdays. There was always work to be done.

In the evenings Martin and Jane rode around the moorland sheep. Shepherds Hill had a hundred roaming the moor. Anything might happen to them. A ewe might go lame. A lamb might be lost. An old ewe might be turned on its back and unable to get up.

On Saturdays they rode around the sheep in the morning, the ponies in the afternoon. Many of the ponies in this corner of the moor belonged to Jane's father. Some of the mares had foals at foot. Others were still fat. Jane didn't disturb them in their quiet valleys. She stood in the stirrups and counted, knowing how many there should be.

In theory these ponies could roam the whole moor; an area about the size of Greater London.

But Jane knew that when they were near foaling, the mares came back to the valleys where they had been born. She found seven in one valley, nine in another. They were cropping near the streams, where the grass was sweetest. They felt the approach of saddle ponies and looked up, more curious than startled.

They were curious about the saddle ponies, not about the people. They were used to people. Every summer hundreds of tourists found their way to this corner of the moor; their cars bouncing off the road to green grass and settling down for picnics.

The oldest mares recognized the picnic signs and came to the cars, begging at the windows, touting for sympathy. To the older mares, with no pride to lose, people in cars meant chocolate biscuits and cake and lumps of sugar. Official signs warned visitors not to feed the ponies. But the old custom persisted. The visitors liked it. So did the mares. There was nothing officialdom could do about it as long as the mares kept begging.

But saddle-ponies were different. They meant riders, and riders in the quiet valleys could mean a threat. The wild ponies looked up, waiting to see what the riders would do.

Jane could recognize her father's by their colour markings. Martin thought most of them looked exactly alike. But she recognized the white spot on a wither or above a foot. Most of the Harvey herd had white markings because of the black and white stallion.

She counted quickly. Seven mares and four foals. There should be another. She looked among the litter of granite rocks, then to the bracken. The twitch of a tail showed where it was. Then she counted again to be sure.

Martin noticed what was happening in the valley. The mares were moving. They knew they were being watched, that this watching was in some way a threat to their freedom. Their heads were down, pretending to be grazing. But they were moving quietly, away from the threat on the hill. They were as sly, as apparently innocent, as a shoplifter preparing to escape.

Tuppence nuckered. The chestnut bumped her jealously, reminding her that she already had company, that she didn't need these beggars on the moor.

Tuppence ignored the bump. She nuckered again, her head sharply etched, her nostrils flaring.

The ragged mares pretended not to hear. Their silent creep did not seem to quicken. You did not realize how quick it was until they were as small as toys. Then they were safe again. They could afford to graze seriously.

Tuppence nuckered a last time. It was an imperious sound, commanding them to answer. She was as indignant as a Princess who rings a bell in an empty house. Even the chestnut knew she was wasting her time.

It was not jealous now. It was impatient. It bumped her again, telling her that she could not stand all day calling ragamuffins who did not want to hear.

Jane showed Martin how many foals so far. She

opened and closed her right hand. Seventeen so far. Before the end of the month there would be twice as many. April and May were the months for foaling on the moor.

They rode to another valley. There were more mares near the stream; no different from mares in other valleys in their sly pretences. But Tuppence's reaction was different. She did not nucker. She turned in sudden jerks, gazing to all corners of the valley. Martin felt her trembling. He spoke and patted. She threw up her head, rejecting his hand, his voice.

Jane saw the danger and shouted. She reached for a rein, but the filly was too quick.

Tuppence was on her knees before Martin realized. His first instinct was to jump. He knew she was going to roll. But if she rolled, she would break the saddle. So he stayed on, pulling her up.

Tuppence stood a moment, angry with frustration. The chestnut felt her mood and turned around and around, fighting the bit. Jane shouted again. Tuppence galloped towards the stream, scattering the wild mares.

Jane sent the chestnut in pursuit, taking a straight line, guessing what Tuppence wanted to do. She didn't ask the chestnut to jump the stream. It was too wide, too shallow. She splashed through and pulled the pony round, coming between Tuppence and the mares.

Tuppence stopped. Again she looked around the valley. Again she wanted to roll.

Martin didn't understand, but Jane waved and pointed. She was pointing to the valley, then to

Tuppence. Now Martin understood. This was the valley where Tuppence had been born. She remembered it. She was celebrating.

'Phew,' Jane said, coming alongside. 'Keep her away from here. Next time she might break your neck.'

Martin darted Jane a glance, trusting her not to tell his mother. Mrs. Manningham always took their adventures seriously, horrified by what might have happened. Though it never does, Martin thought. Nothing is ever as bad as parents imagine. They forget the excitement and see only the dangers.

But once he was frightened. He was riding alone from Grannie's store. One second Tuppence was jogging, thinking of home and bran; the next she had whipped round and was staring towards the skyline. Her head was high. Her nostrils were as wide and round as trumpets.

He felt that at any moment she would throw him. He gripped with his knees, shortening the reins. He knew she had forgotten him. She was thinking of whatever she had seen or heard. He looked towards the skyline, trying to see what she had seen. He saw it; a movement, a flicker of black and white like the flight of a magpie. But this was no magpie. This was the black and white of Harvey's piebald stallion.

He watched the stallion run in and out of the rocks on the hill. It was swanking, tossing its head and arching its neck. He guessed that it was calling. Its tail was out. Its mane was blowing like a battle flag.

He kept Tuppence still, waiting for the stallion to pass beyond the rocks and over the skyline. He didn't understand what had almost happened, but he knew there had been a crisis and that he had almost lost.

For perhaps five minutes Tuppence watched the skyline, waiting for the stallion to come back. Then she relaxed. All the tension went out of her and she became his again. They were home in time for supper and for the homework which always followed supper.

Homework was in two parts; the subjects he liked and the subjects he hated. He spent an hour on subjects he liked, five minutes on the others.

History, for instance. 'Describe a Norman castle.' He could do better than that. He could describe a siege; one army attacking, the other defending; one attacking with arrows, with boulders slung from a giant sling; the other conserving their ammunition, their food, resolved never to surrender. He made this the most important subject of the evening. He skipped the decimals.

His mother knew he was skipping. She made him do a full exercise, although he tried tiredness and Miss-Powell-said-we-needn't and that old standby, a splitting headache.

Easy in most things, his mother was strict about homework. She wanted him to 'get on'; to earn a good report at the end of the school year. She wanted to be proud when she talked to the school staff about him.

She even made him try lip-reading, insisting that he would like it as soon as he became proficient.

Martin doubted it. Lip-reading now was what physical education had been at primary school; something you missed if you could.

He guessed that his father would let him off, but when it came to the test, Mr. Manningham was always hiding behind the newspaper. He wouldn't appear again until his wife had got her way and Martin was trying.

She sat with the light on her face, keeping her voice low in a conversational way, letting her expressions emphasize what the words were saying.

At first Martin had strained to see every word. Now he tried to guess. He watched for a word in the middle or at the end of a sentence, then guessed the rest. Sometimes he was absurdly wrong. Then his mother repeated it, acting with her face and hands to explain the meaning.

Questions were the easiest. When she asked, 'What are you going to do tomorrow?' he recognized 'what' and 'tomorrow' and guessed by the lift of her eyebrows that she was asking a question. Then, when she pointed at him, he knew she meant 'you' and could fill in the rest.

He was making progress, if only slowly. She thought any progress was wonderful. But he knew that compared with others in his class he was backward. They could 'listen' by 'looking' for long periods, but he was soon exhausted and exasperated.

His mother encouraged him to watch the B.B.C. television programmes for the deaf. The subjects were interesting, but the manner of presentation emphasized that the deaf were different. There was a determined niceness about the television faces, like being nice to half-wits.

Martin always felt stupid as he watched. The faces were making a special effort for him. He knew they were doing their best to help and please him, but still he couldn't understand all of it. That showed how stupid he must be.

To his surprise he found that his favourite television programme was the Sunday evening service. He liked watching the solo singers. They shaped the words, giving him a chance yet not doing it because they wanted to give him a chance. When he recognized a word or two of a hymn, he could call on memory to help recognize the rest.

Sometimes his mother joined the singing. Then his father joined, too, singing seriously because he was proud of his deep voice. They smiled as they sang, encouraging him to try.

He couldn't. He guessed it would be a terrible row and that they wouldn't tell him.

Jane helped in another way. She liked pop groups on television, imitating the way they played guitars and drums. Her excitement encouraged Martin to take part.

She played a home-made guitar. He played drums made from wooden boxes, with saucepan-lids for cymbals. He watched the television drummer and imitated without hearing, delighted by the feeling of din. He and Jane took over the parlour, thumping out their private noises, sharing their excitement with the professional faces on the screen.

They were playing the evening before the disaster.

Jane strummed and Martin thumped, while Mr. and Mrs. Manningham tried to guess which pop group they were imitating now. Jane's favourites were Freddie and the Dreamers. Martin liked the Rolling Stones. Mr. Manningham guessed one, his wife the other, although it didn't matter.

Martin showed them. He got up from the drums and imitated Freddie's absurd, good-humoured dance, legs bent and heels kicking. Martin was laughing, all his shyness gone.

'Freddie,' his mother cried.

Then Jane joined in the silly, laughing dance. They jigged around the room, making it a merry evening.

There was still no hint of the disaster to come.

Jane left for home as the sky began to forget the sun. Her chestnut was stabled in Tuppence's box.

Martin came from the house to watch her saddle and mount and turn for home. The chestnut was keen to go, knowing there would be corn and bran waiting. Mrs. Manningham asked Jane to wait a minute.

She brought out a jar of home-made chutney, giving it to Jane, saying 'For your mother.' It was more than a gesture between neighbours. It was a way of thanking Jane for encouraging Martin to drum and dance and forget his deafness.

Jane slipped the jar into a pocket, bulging her coat. She raised a hand to Martin and he answered. They had learned to talk by signals. Jauntily the chestnut went down the hill and over the bridge. So far it was still a merry evening.

Martin went to the orchard, where Tuppence

was watching and listening, following the departure of the chestnut. He gave her a carrot. She listened and nudged, then listened again.

So far there was no reason for alarm.

It was late, half past eight; although it seemed much earlier than half past eight had been in the darkness of January. Martin gave her a final slap and returned to the house.

In the porch he looked over his shoulder. She was looking out to the moor. Her rigid listening told him she could hear something. But still he was not alarmed. He thought she was listening to the faraway sounds of the chestnut.

By nine o'clock he was in bed, too tired to read. In five minutes he was asleep.

He did not wake up until the morning. By then it was too late.

# CHAPTER EIGHT

IT was Sunday. Martin knew it as soon as he opened his eyes. Sunday had a special feel. No school, no urgency, no need to hurry. He could stretch and watch the sunshine buttering the wall.

The sunshine made the day something to celebrate. He got up, looking from the window. The colours of the moor were the green of grass and bracken, the yellow of gorse. The shadows were deep purple near the granite rocks.

It was still cold, but the sun promised that this cold was only a beginning. By eleven o'clock the day would be grown up. The sun would have won.

He reached for his shirt and jersey and jodhpurs. He looked forward to riding with Jane. The ponies would feel the gaiety of the morning. Tuppence would be eager. Martin hurried, feeling sure that Jane would recognize the promise in such sunshine and would be already coming to meet him.

He went to the landing and stopped. His mother was coming up the stairs. She pointed to his clothes, shaking her head, making them the wrong clothes. She came nearer, compelling him to turn and go back to his room.

She took his suit from the wardrobe. It meant

church. She turned the bathroom taps, filling the basin. That meant washing.

He couldn't believe his luck. He sat on the bed, sulking, mourning the wasted sunshine. He watched her face, hoping for some sign of relenting.

Her face was pale and tense. She wouldn't look at him. She opened drawers, bringing out his best shirt, his grey socks and best tie.

'What's the matter?' he asked. 'Why can't I ride with Jane? Why can't we go to church this evening?'

She didn't answer. She made him wash, brush his teeth, comb his hair. When he combed it to his eyebrows in the fashionable way, she brushed it across, pretending she'd never heard of the Rolling Stones.

It was more than the usual fussing before church. She kept glancing to the window. Now and again she stopped, thinking of something. She seemed to be listening.

He thought she was frightened, then dismissed it. The day was Sunday. Sunday wasn't a day to frighten anyone.

He said, 'It's never fair. Jane won't have to go.'

She found a white handkerchief, insisted that he tied the tie properly and made bows of his shoelaces. He felt persecuted. For five minutes he wished he lived with the Harveys. They wouldn't dress him up on a sunshine morning. They'd let him go free, wearing old clothes and getting as dirty as he liked.

He said, 'I wish I lived with the Harvey's'; hoping to hurt her, to show her how serious it was.

She didn't seem to hear. She beckoned him to the landing, making going to church urgent, as though they were already late.

He went down the stairs, hoping Jane would be there. Perhaps Jane would appeal for him, convincing his mother that this was an ideal morning for riding.

But Jane was not there. Neither was his father.

He was surprised. Mr. Manningham should be there because it was his Sunday morning off. He and Nathan worked alternate Sundays, feeding and milking. This was Nathan's morning.

Martin saw the farm-hand come from the shippen. So where was his father and why the haste, the feeling that his mother was hiding something?

He drew a chair to the table, guessing answers to the questions. Perhaps it was nothing. Perhaps his father had gone to Grannie's store for the Sunday papers. It could be as simple as that. His mother gave him breakfast; sausage and egg, toast and marmalade, coffee thick with cream. He chased a bubble round the surface of the coffee. He made up his mind to sulk throughout the service. That would show her.

Mrs. Manningham pushed salt and pepper towards him, then dashed up the stairs to change and do her hair and put on her Sunday hat.

He still couldn't understand the haste. Usually she took a long time getting ready for church.

He ate miserably, grumbling to himself. There was only one consolation. There would be time to go to the orchard and explain it to Tuppence. She'd be as indignant as he was. She'd understand that it was a waste of the best sunshine of the spring.

He got up, leaving most of the toast and marmalade. But as he moved from the table his mother was there. She must have been listening, waiting for the scrape-back of his chair. She had fled down the stairs, still struggling with her hat.

'Where are you going?'

He pretended not to understand. He continued towards the porch, but his mother was there first. She barred the way, refusing to let him pass.

'You can't, there isn't time.'

The clock said there was. He could have five minutes with his pony and still be in church before eleven.

'No, you mustn't. Your clothes, your shoes. The orchard mud, it would spoil your shoes.'

Poor reasons. He didn't mind dirty shoes and he couldn't leave without explaining to Tuppence.

He would have gone, pushing past her to the door, but Nathan was there. Nathan and his mother exchanged frightened glances. His mother was asking for help.

Sternly Nathan said, 'You do what you're told. You got to go to church.'

Martin was crestfallen. Nathan had never looked so stern. There was no merriment now in his pale blue eyes. They were like chips of ice.

He began to say, 'I know, I'm going. I only want to see Tuppence . . .'

Nathan didn't move from the doorway. He said,

'You must do what your mother says. You mustn't push ...'

Martin tried to explain. He hadn't meant to push, he wouldn't hurt his mother. It was just so silly, when there was plenty of time.

'There's always a reason,' Nathan said.

Now Mrs. Manningham was ready. She was pulling on her gloves, remembering her hymn book, the silver for the collection. Martin went with her to the car.

Nathan opened the door for her. She turned her head, saying something to him, refusing to let Martin see her face. Nathan nodded and slammed the door. He came around to Martin's side, making sure the door was secure. He winked. Martin understood what the wink said. They were friends again.

He looked back to the orchard as the car moved down the hill. He saw only the trees. He glanced a protest, asking his mother to drive slowly, to let him see his pony. But she seemed not to notice.

She gave all her attention to driving. She didn't drive often. She hated it. She had learned to drive only because she might be needed in an emergency.

Martin remembered his father. He said, 'Where's Dad? I thought he'd gone for the papers.'

She threw him a frightened glance, then muttered something, anything. He remembered that something had been missing from a corner of the yard.

He said, 'Has he gone somewhere in the Land

Rover? Where then? What can be so important on a Sunday morning?'

The car reached the highway and turned towards the nearest hamlet. A hundred years ago moorland farmers had ridden to church, with their wives riding pillion behind. Martin had seen old drawings. The pace had been a steady plod, and services had been held in the afternoons to give the farmers time to get to church and home again in daylight.

Going to church then had been the first duty on a Sunday. Even storms and snow had not discouraged them. Now it was much easier. Cars travelled long distances in half an hour. Yet few moorland people made the effort, except at Christmas and Easter, with harvest festival the big service of the year.

Martin thought that was why his mother made the effort. Morning congregations were often pitifully small, made up almost entirely of retired people who had come to old cottages and new bungalows. She believed that farmers and their families should find time once a week to give thanks for the miracles of birth and growth, for the annual magic of spring.

The church was small. Its tower was as tall as a prophet. Around it were the gravestones of other generations. Martin knew that some of these gravestones were his father's parents and grandparents and great-grandparents; that over there, beyond the yew tree, were his mother's father and uncles.

He had seen photographs of some of them. Once these gravestones had been men, big and bearded and immensely solemn and strong. Once the women had worn long skirts and white aprons and strange little white caps. They had worked long days. They had carried water from the well; made butter and hogs pudding; ploughed two acres a day behind old horses.

The great festival of their year had been Christmas, when all members of the family had come together for hot cider and goose and plumpudding, for old songs in the firelight.

No television then, Martin thought. No radio to tell Dartmoor of what was happening in China and Brazil. All the gossip had been about the family. All the firelit stories had been about ghosts and superstition, while the songs had been inherited, passed down from mother to children.

Martin remembered one of the songs. His mother had sung it when he was small. It was a song of many verses, mentioning moorland names which had lived once but had been forgotten long ago. She had got it from her mother. Now he remembered some of the lines, surprised to find them still there in the corner of memory.

The car drew up near the church. They were much too early. Martin knew that because their car was the first. Usually it was among the last.

He said, 'I told you so,' but his mother was reaching to the back seat for flowers and scissors. She was going to the graves. Perhaps that was why they had come early. But why hadn't she explained? Why had she been so frightened?

He followed her to the gravestones; to Grandfather Manningham and Grandfather Jordan because Jordan had been her maiden name. He helped her empty the vases of dead flowers and sour water. Then the vases were re-sunk in their earth-holes and fresh water was poured in. He picked up the litter of dead leaves and carried them to a wire basket.

The litter basket was near the wall which divided the church-yard and the moor. He looked up, surprised by the sudden movement on the moor. It was a black and white movement. He recognized Harvey's stallion. It was running strongly, its white mane and tail streaming. He knew it was being chased. He watched the skyline, waiting for other ponies to show.

Two came over the skyline. He recognized Jane, then Harvey. He wondered why they were driving the stallion and where. Usually the stallion ran with the mares until the end of June.

He turned to call his mother. She had straightened from the grave. She had seen. Her fright was back.

They watched the stallion turn from the hamlet and the threat of people. It returned to the granite rocks on the skyline. It disappeared. Soon Jane and her father were dots that faded as you watched.

'Why?' Martin asked. 'What's the matter? What's happened?'

Mrs. Manningham shook her head, brushing away the questions. She kept him busy, tidying the litter, fetching water from the tap, cutting the grass of Grandfather Jordan's grave.

Other people were coming up the path to church. They spoke and she answered, the usual pleasantries about the weather. But she did not stop working. It seemed that being busy was a kind of protection, giving her less time to think.

Martin's bewilderment became resentment. Why was she worried, frightened, pecking quick glances to the moor? Why didn't she explain? Why couldn't she say?

'There.' She straightened from the grave, brushing earth from her fingers. 'I wanted to finish it. Now let's go in.'

Outside the church seemed small in the shadow of the moor. Inside it seemed huge because there were so few people. Two in the front pew, three over there, two near the pillar. Martin counted eleven as he passed up the centre aisle.

His mother stepped into the pew which her parents and grandparents had used. The hassocks were old and had limp flaps. Martin thought the flaps were chewed, like the ears of fighting terriers.

He knelt for the minute of private prayer before the service began. He saw his mother rest her elbows on the book-rest and cover her face with gloved hands. He wondered what she was praying.

Then he closed his eyes and said his own prayer; not aloud but privately. 'Please God look after Tuppence and thank you for letting me have her and I promise to take good care of her always . . .'

His prayer was finished. He was ready to sit back and wait for the service to begin. But his mother did not sit back. She knelt a long time, still covering her face. He felt again that she was hiding something,

something terrible; that she was praying about this something terrible, asking God to help. He watched her face when at last she lowered her hands and sat back. It was stained with tears.

His resentment melted. He was ashamed of his sulkiness. He tucked a hand in her arm, watching the tear stains, thinking he knew why his mother had cried.

Something had happened to Grannie Jordan. That would explain the tears and his father's absence. Perhaps Grannie had died in the night.

The service began. Usually he followed it in the prayer-book, reading as the curate spoke, with his mother's finger pointing to the responses. Now he could not see the words. He stared at the opened book, wondering why his mother had not told him, had not explained; why she had made a secret of it.

It was a dull service. The sermon seemed as long as tooth-ache. Of the hymns he knew the tune of only one: 'Oh God, our help in ages past . . .'

His mother sang it. Her nudge asked him to join in. But he couldn't, the sound wouldn't come. The church seemed cold and miserable because there were so few to sing.

The service ended. The people rose from their knees and came down the centre aisle towards the south door. Mrs. Manningham paused a minute in the porch, exchanging how-are-you's? with those she knew best. One or two of the women glanced to Martin as they talked. He hoped they were not talking about him.

He fretted on the step of the porch, begging his

mother to come. He wanted to ask the question which would end his doubts. He wanted to ask, 'Why didn't you tell me about Grannie?'

But when they were in the car and he asked the question, she seemed startled. She shook her head, telling him it wasn't Grannie.

'What then? You were crying, so what can it be then?'

She tried to smile, pretending that her tears had been silly, meaning nothing. She turned the car for home, but Martin noticed that the nearer they came to Shepherds Hill, the slower she drove. She always drove cautiously, but this was more than caution. It was fear.

He saw that she was afraid to reach Shepherds Hill because of something which had happened there.

He asked himself, 'When could anything have happened?' And the answer was immediate. In the night.

Then he asked himself, 'What could have happened to be so serious?' And suddenly the answer was there, although he didn't want to hear it.

He watched her quick glances to the moor; looking for someone, half-hoping, half-fearing.

He saw her look to the orchard as the car crossed the bridge and came up the slope. He saw her speak to Nathan at the gate; then to his father when he came to the yard. Their faces told him what the secret was.

He had the door open before the car stopped. He struggled out, shaking off his mother's hand, pushing aside his father. He swerved to avoid Nathan and ran up the lane.

He reached the orchard. He called. He looked through the trees, begging her to come. He climbed over the gate to the mud on the other side. He knew the search was hopeless.

He knew the orchard was empty.

His father and Nathan were waiting in the yard. They came towards him, trying to explain.

It had happened in the night. Tuppence had jumped the wall, escaping to the moor.

Martin shook his head, unable to believe it.

'Not her fault,' Nathan said. 'It's nature, see. It's the time of the year. That black and white stallion was calling.'

Martin remembered how the stallion had called when they were returning from Grannie's store. He remembered Tuppence's excitement. He had almost lost her then.

'Look,' his father said. 'She isn't lost, not forever. She's somewhere on the moor.'

A picture came into Martin's head. He remembered Jane and her father driving the stallion. Presumably they'd been looking for Tuppence. Presumably they'd known what had happened – long before he had.

He flashed, 'You didn't tell me, you made me go to church.'

His father pointed to the Land Rover. 'I had been out all the morning, looking for her. Harvey and Jane and the other farmers. They've been helping. As soon as I found out, I 'phoned round and they all did what they could.'

'But where is she?'

Mr. Manningham shook his head. They'd found the stallion. They'd found other mares. But there had been no sign of Tuppence.

'She might have gone miles,' Nathan said. 'Twenty miles, even more.'

Martin began to ask, 'Why didn't you tell me? I could have helped ...' But he knew the answer. They had hoped to have Tuppence back in the orchard before his return from church.

His father put a hand on his shoulder. 'You go this afternoon, you and Jane. Perhaps you'll be luckier than we were.'

Martin ran to change into old clothes and gumboots. He shook his head to his mother's protests about dinner, impatient for his father to 'phone Jane.

'She'll bring over a spare pony for you,' Mr. Manningham said. 'She's been a trump, that maid.'

Martin trusted Jane to hurry. He ran to the bridge to wait. She came across the moor, riding the chestnut and leading a skewbald.

He clambered up on the brown and white pony, and they turned away to the secret places on the moor.

'The valleys,' Jane called. 'We'll try them all.'

At first their optimism was high. They felt sure they would succeed where the men had failed this morning. But as each valley proved a failure, their optimism went down and down to despair.

The ponies were tired. Martin did not want to stop to rest them, but Jane made him get down and slacken the girths and let the skewbald graze.

He sat beside her on a boulder, shaking his head to her sandwiches. He couldn't eat. The idea of eating made a lump in his throat. He could only see the pictures in his head.

The pictures were all of Tuppence and what might have happened. He imagined her galloping wildly across a road and being hit by a car.

Jane glanced at her watch. She got up, giving what was left of the sandwiches to the ponies. They ate jealously, the chestnut wanting more than the skewbald.

Martin fretted, begrudging every minute. He didn't see the joke. Now he was impatient of Jane petting the ponies as a few weeks ago Jane had been impatient of him petting Tuppence.

'Where now?' Jane asked.

They searched thick plantations, hoping Tuppence had found shelter among trees. They looked among the rocks of the highest tors, thinking that if Tuppence had galloped all night, she might be lying there. They came to a ridge, looking down to a green valley. It was empty. There was no hint of movement.

'There were mares here yesterday,' Jane said.

She was surprised, suspicious. She looked across the bracken and gorse to the running light of the stream.

Her suspicions deepened. The silence was too complete. She beckoned Martin down the slope.

The ponies crept. Her chestnut hesitated,

throwing its head and stiffening its forelegs. It didn't want to go on. Immediately the skewbald caught the reluctance. For a while both ponies refused to budge.

'There's something here,' Jane said.

She glanced around the bracken. It could be a snake, an adder. But the tremor of the ponies' nostrils suggested they were smelling something.

She got down and Martin followed. The ponies stared fixedly down the hill.

There were boulders in the stream. They were as big as seals. The water pottered around them, talking to itself. There seemed no reason for the ponies' reluctance.

Martin passed his reins to Jane and went down the slope. At first he hurried. Then his feet slowed, his legs became heavy. He was afraid of what he would find.

The bracken near the stream was crushed. The turf was scratched as though something had dragged itself towards the stream.

His mouth was dry. His heart was hammering. He came down the last slope, a sudden slipping descent. He reached the stream and saw what the boulder was hiding.

# CHAPTER NINE

TUPPENCE lay on her side in the shallow stream. There were black stains on her neck and wither. The stains rose with a buzz and tried to come back. He realized they were flies. His hand punched, driving them away.

He thought she was dead.

He stepped into the stream. It was so shallow that it did not cover the toes of his boots. The stones beneath were as smooth as a miser's pennies.

Her head was tilted, so that the water ran beneath her chin, trailing the long hairs like black weeds Her eye was open but he still thought she was dead. Animals did not close their eyes in death. He had learned that on the farm.

He spoke her name, gently, like mourning the dead. She heard. Her eye answered. He saw the recognition and dropped on a knee.

His hands touched her, one keeping away the flies while the other talked. All right, his hand said. We've found you. We've been looking everywhere.

He saw why the flies wanted her. There were ragged marks on her neck and wither. They might have been torn by teeth.

He remembered Jane and looked up the hill. He waved, beckoning her down. She dropped the reins, trusting the ponies to graze without wandering. She came down the slope, hurrying as he had hurried, then slowing as he had slowed.

Martin said, 'She's been bitten. Here, look, and here.'

Jane crept nearer. She looked a long time at the teeth wounds, then back to Martin.

She knew the pony would not lie like that because of teeth wounds. The marks on her neck and wither were not as bad as that. Ointment for a month would heal them and new hair would cover the scars. Within a year you wouldn't be able to find where the marks had been.

Jane guessed it must be something else. She crouched. She ran her hands down the pony's legs, feeling for a break. They were cold from the running water.

She said, 'Her legs are all right.'

She tried to smile, making it good news. But she knew there must be something else. She splashed to join Martin at the pony's head.

Tuppence heard her coming and moved, lifting her head from the water. Jane saw it then. Martin saw it, too.

They saw the other side of her head. The water took away wisps of blood which had broken with the movement.

Jane flinched, glancing in astonishment to Martin. He was white. His face was pinched and ill.

Abruptly Jane said, 'She'll die for sure.' She

meant it kindly, an assurance that quick death would end the pain.

They knelt in the water like kneeling at a grave. They were appalled by what had happened to her head.

Then Martin looked up to the skyline, thinking of Shepherds Hill and how far it was and if his father could come in time. He touched Jane's arm and pointed.

She hesitated, then stood up. All right, she'd do what she could. Even though help might come too late.

She caught the chestnut easily and swung to the saddle. The skewbald ran alongside, but she brandished her stick, driving it away. It realized that it could graze if it wanted and dropped its head.

Jane dug her heels and the chestnut responded, supposing that it was going home. But she would not let it take the homeward road. She turned it towards Shepherds Hill and for a hundred yards the chestnut shook its head in protest, trying to turn the way it knew best.

'Come on,' Jane shouted, bringing down her stick.

Mrs. Manningham saw her coming and called to the farmer. He was at the gate as Jane reached it. He knew by her face that it was bad.

'The side of her head,' Jane said.

Mr. Manningham groaned.

'She's in the stream,' Jane said. 'The cold water has stopped the bleeding.'

He glanced to his wife, asking her to fetch the gun.

'Blackcherry stream,' Jane said. 'Martin's still with her.'

Mrs. Manningham brought the gun. He held out the other hand. She gave him the cartridges.

Martin watched the skyline, waiting for his father. He began to realize what had happened. His little filly had brought her terrible wounds to this stream, instinctively aware that the cold and running water would stem the bleeding.

Then he realized something else. He recognized the valley. This was where she had become excited, had tried to roll, had run among the mares. This was where she had been born.

In the blind reasoning of pain, Tuppence had struggled back to the valley which she remembered best.

It's all right, his hand kept saying. Meanwhile his eyes watched the skyline, waiting for his father.

Mr. Manningham crossed the skyline with Jane and Nathan. They were hurrying. Martin guessed that they had come as far as possible by Land Rover. They stumbled down the hill, growing bigger as he watched.

It's all right, his hand said. My father's coming.

His father was near the stream before he saw the gun. He stood up. The movement disturbed the water. For a second it lapped over the pony's nostrils.

Tuppence moved her head, straining to keep her nostrils free. The straining released those wisps of red, as long as ribbons. He pushed out his hands, telling his father to stand back.

Mr. Manningham came to the stream. His expression was determined. Martin guessed the gun was loaded.

Mr. Manningham crouched beside Tuppence. He put a hand to the under side of her nose. His touch was gentle. He turned her head. He saw it and glanced to Nathan. The shake of his head was slight.

Martin saw it. He lunged at his father, pushing the gun aside. He shouted, 'No.' He shouted it again and again.

Nathan touched him, trying to persuade him. Come away, leave it to your father. It's got to be done. That's what the touch was saying.

Martin brushed the hand away, not taking his eyes from his father. He said, 'If you touch her, if you dare touch her . . .'

His father tried to explain. 'Look, you can't let a pony suffer. Look, she's dying, it's best to end it now.'

'You dare,' Martin said.

His father's distress became anger. Martin couldn't understand the shouting, but he knew what his father's face was saying. 'Do you think I want to? Do you think I use a gun because I like it?'

Nathan's hand closed on the boy's arm. The grip was firm. It tightened when Martin struggled.

'Come away,' Nathan said. 'It'll be over in a second.'

Martin hit the hand which held him. His

strength was small compared with Nathan's.

'Sometimes you got to,' Mr. Manningham said. 'You got to do things you hate.'

Martin threw an appeal to Jane, begging her to say something, do something. He saw her saying something, pointing to him, then to the pony, pleading with his father.

The gestures seemed to be saying, 'Let him try...'

His father hesitated. Martin saw he was surprised that even Jane thought the pony might be saved.

'We can't get her back,' Mr. Manningham said. 'We daren't move her.'

'My father's horse-box,' Jane said. 'It's got a low ramp. We can get her up. And bales of straw on either side to hold her upright.'

Mr. Manningham looked up to the sky, judging how much daylight was left. Martin saw the decision come into his face. If they were going to do something, they must hurry. The horse-box must be here before dark. Someone must telephone the vet.

He nodded to Nathan. The farm-hand moved away at once, turning in the direction of Harvey's farm. He would telephone from there, then bring Harvey with the horse-box.

'And a hurdle,' Mr. Manningham called. 'We'll need it if Harvey can't get the horse-box near enough.'

He realized that he still held the gun. Carefully he put it down. He watched the boy's eyes, remembering the blaze of hatred.

Gently he said, 'We'll do everything we can. We'll look after this little pony like she was the finest racehorse in the world.'

Martin didn't understand the words, but he understood the gentleness. He half-smiled, not trusting his voice to answer.

'But don't hope for too much,' Mr. Manningham said. 'There's a limit to what even the best vets can do.'

The veterinary surgeon was Irish. He had recently arrived in the neighbourhood and was known to be good with horses. He looked up to the anxious faces.

Carefully he explained there was a faint hope. While life remained there must be a faint hope. But any treatment would be slow and expensive.

'It'll cost you money.' The vet waited, then added firmly, 'More than the little lady's worth.'

Mr. Manningham felt his son watching. He said, 'Never – mind what she's worth. Is there a chance?'

The vet repeated what he had said. There must always be a chance.

'A reasonable chance?' Mr. Manningham said.

The vet hesitated, then shook his head. 'This little lady's worth – what? Thirty pounds? Modern drugs can do more than would have seemed possible even ten years ago. But they cost money. She'd need treatment four times a day. By the end of a month, you'd have a big bill. By the end of three months. . . .'

The suggestion was that by the end of three

months the bill would be higher than the farmer would be willing to pay.

'I told you,' Mr. Manningham said. 'Never mind the money.'

The vet gave him a long look, then glanced to the boy. Mr. Manningham didn't nod, but his eyes answered.

'All right,' the vet said, 'As long as it's understood. It might be a month with nothing to show. Then she might still have to be put down.'

'It's understood,' Mr. Manningham said.

The vet looked up to Martin. 'I'll need help. Not just one day but every day.'

Martin didn't speak. He met the vet's eyes in a long stare.

'All right then,' the vet said. 'As long as you realize. There's no quick results with animals.'

Nathan helped the vet do what could be done at once. Mr. Manningham took Jane and Martin away, their backs turned so they could not see.

Jane asked, 'It wasn't the stallion did that, was it?'

Mr. Manningham shook his head. The stallion's bites were on her neck and wither, but the injuries to her head had not been inflicted by the stallion.

'By the mares,' he said.

Other mares of the herd had turned in jealousy on the stranger, stunning her down, then hammering their fore-feet in a dance of jealous rage. That was what could happen to a pony which smelled of men and of captivity if it tried to rejoin the moorland community.

Martin prayed. Years ago he had been taught to say bedtime prayers. It had been part of preparing himself for sleep. But when he was eight or nine, something had happened. He'd lost the habit of nightly prayers, not suddenly but slowly. He'd begun to confuse God with the vicar, who was dry and dull and who preached long sermons. Since then he had prayed only when his mother insisted. His prayers had become polite and formal, rattled through in quicker and quicker time.

It was different now. His bedside prayer was long and private and muddled. It kept saying 'Please'. It was the sort of prayer you could repeat at all times of the day, standing or sitting, even when others were looking.

His mother saw the distress. She whispered, 'It was a mistake. The gun would have been quicker.'

His father flashed an answer. 'Perhaps it would, but not me. Not my finger on the trigger.'

The vet came to the kitchen for a glass of whisky before he left. For a while they chatted socially. Mrs. Manningham asked how he liked working on Dartmoor. He made a joke of the weather.

Then he said, 'There's a limit to what I can do. I can do so much. The rest is up to that boy. I can show him what to do, but I can't show him how to be patient, how to keep trying when he's tired and fed up.'

Mrs. Manningham saw what it might mean to Martin. He would have to find time before and after school. He would soon be tired out. She glanced a protest, but her husband seemed not to notice.

He said, 'You can trust the boy. He'll do anything to save that little pony.'

'Anything?' the vet said.

'Anything,' Mr. Manningham answered.

# CHAPTER TEN

TUPPENCE didn't fret or protest. She was frighteningly quiet. She drank a little, but would not eat.

Martin tempted her with carrot and sugar, making a game of it, biting part of the carrot to show what she was missing.

But Tuppence showed no interest. Once, when she took a piece and held it a moment, she let it out again as though to move her bottom jaw in a crunching movement was too much.

She stood in the middle of the box, her front feet apart, her head down in dejection. She was suffering great pain without sound. Her silence was noble and lonely.

Martin thought she was ashamed of her head. She stood with the bad side turned from those who came to see. Martin's pity was too deep for words. He sat in a corner of the box, talking to her, letting his voice be her companion. He talked about the times she had drawn the sledge and outpaced the chestnut and found the way through the bog. Always he implied that those days were not ended. They were only postponed. Soon she would be galloping again, making them laugh again.

The vet came each morning and evening. At first

he said little to Martin, embarrassed by the boy's deafness. But in the first few weeks their friendship deepened.

The vet saw that the boy was serious and determined, that he could be trusted to do all he promised. He told him one of the secrets of treating animals – time. That was the important word. Give a young, strong animal time and privacy, and none knew what miracle might happen.

'Never interfere,' he said. 'Never meddle. Do what must be done, then let nature do the rest.'

Martin liked the way he touched Tuppence. His touch made her more than a pony. She became his patient, as important as the richest patient in a hospital. He called her 'little lady'.

'A game little lady,' the vet said. 'She won't give in easy.'

Martin was proud of the praise. He knew in his heart she would never hunt again nor win rosettes at shows or gymkhanas. She'd never win prizes anywhere. But to earn such praise from one who did not praise easily, that was a kind of winning.

He added his own praise, not in words but with his hands. She leaned into him and this leaning was a sign of how much she depended on him. Their relationship had changed. Not long ago he had depended on her. She had been his ears. Her instinct had got him out of Crockin Bog. Now she leaned, making him the nurse. She'd become the invalid.

He responded to it. Her dependence deepened his responsibility, and responsibility was important to him. He read the vet's changing instructions and obeyed every word. He was out of bed at six to tend the wounds before breakfast. Then, as soon as he returned from school, he was in the stable again, repeating the treatment before tea.

After tea there was homework. His mother would not let him off that, although he wriggled.

But at nine o'clock he was doing it all again, not bored or tired by the repetition. His reward was the vet's praise. He could see little change but the vet said the pony was fighting back. That assurance had to be enough.

'You're tiring yourself out,' his mother said. 'You're always late to bed. It's been over a month and never to bed on time.'

He pretended that early to bed was kids' stuff, but sometimes in school his eyes were heavy. He could not concentrate. His brain wouldn't give the answers to simple sums.

Miss Powell watched him anxiously. She knew what he was doing because his essays and daily diary informed her. The diary had in fact become a monotonous record of his daily routine in the stable. It seemed that he had neither time nor thought for anything else.

'You're tired,' she said, touching him.

He shrugged the hands away. He was ashamed of his tiredness, making it a kind of weakness. He knew that if a young, healthy animal could survive great pain, a young, healthy boy could survive much more than some adults believed.

He guessed that Miss Powell and his mother had discussed it on the telephone. The school encouraged a strong link between teachers and parents, but in his tiredness he made it a conspiracy. Even Miss Powell, even his mother seemed sure that his efforts were doomed, that Tuppence would never recover.

His father and Nathan were more encouraging. They understood the importance of time, the inevitability of repetition. For the first time he found he could talk to his father more easily than he could talk to his mother. He told him what the vet had said. He asked his father to see some improvement, and Mr. Manningham pretended to see more than was there.

'You're a good lad. You've started something. Now you've got to see it through.'

Martin was determined to see it through. Surely that was more important than not having enough sleep and forgetting where to put the decimal point?

'It's not more important,' his mother said. 'You're getting so touchy. You're falling behind at school.'

One week made a difference. On the 20th of June Tuppence was still an invalid, little better for a month of nursing. On the 27th of June she was moving around the box, looking towards the door and the daylight beyond. She was making it plain that she wanted to go out.

Martin led her to the stream. She could not wear halter or head-collar, so he led her with his fingers in her mane. She liked standing in the sunlit water. She hung her head and dozed while he slapped away the flies.

Horse-flies were easy. One smack and they

dropped to the water. But blow-flies were persistent. They kept coming back.

The change of routine helped Martin as much as the pony. He was still late to bed and early to rise, but the sense of progress lightened the burden. He felt much less tired. He was much less impatient of his mother's concern. He worked well at school. He knew Miss Powell was pleased and relieved.

But soon the half-hour in the stream lost its novelty. It became part of the routine. He tried whistling and looking for fish, but still the half-hour dragged. He began to welcome days of heavy rain. Rain was his excuse for leaving Tuppence in the box.

Now the vet came only once a week. He was trusting Martin to do all that he had promised, and Martin felt the trust and forced himself to accept the routine. But his father and Nathan knew how near he was to giving up.

'Why don't you let him?' Mrs. Manningham said. 'Surely you and Nathan can do most of it.'

Her husband shook his head. 'It's got to be him. He's got to learn what it takes.'

In late July Tuppence was well enough to be turned out. Martin would have taken her to the orchard by day, bringing her in at night. But Nathan advised differently.

'Turn her out at night. No flies then. Flies in the daytime, they'd plague her cruel.'

So Tuppence pottered the orchard in the cool darkness and that was progress. Martin spent the early days in his summer holidays watching over her.

He spent the hot hours in the stable, sitting against a bale of straw, writing stories and drawing with coloured pencils.

All that he wrote was about Tuppence; not as she was in life but as she was in his imagination. In his stories she was a race-horse or show-jumper. Once she won the Grand National. Twice she was judged Pony of the Year. He hid the exercise books, not showing the stories to anyone.

She was also in all that he drew. His favourite scene was an orchard, green branches and brown trunks; and somewhere among the trees there was Tuppence. His green, brown and black pencils were always worn down quicker than the others.

In the cool evening, when Tuppence went out to the orchard, he sat on a fallen tree, reading while the light was good, feeding her carrots when it wasn't.

His mother helped by giving interesting books. Some were bought. Some were borrowed from the county library. The library was a van which travelled the country places.

His favourite books were of other lands. He read about Central Asia, where nomad shepherds used camels for transport and as a source of milk. He was enthralled by Bukhara, an ancient trading centre for silks, spices and jewels. Genghis Khan invaded it and slaughtered all the population, even the children. He read about the animals of Africa and the life story of a salmon.

He passed the best books to Jane, but she wasn't interested. She preferred doing to reading. She didn't expect to pass the eleven-plus and didn't care. Her only ambition was to win rosettes at shows and gymkhanas.

She came regularly during the first fortnight of the holidays, but they learned not to let the chestnut come near Tuppence. It stretched its neck to nose Tuppence in a touch of recognition. Then it smelled the wrong side of her head and flinched, flattening its ears and snapping.

The chestnut condemned Tuppence for her injuries. Martin saw that nature had no sympathy for the wounded.

But before the fortnight was over, Jane was complaining. There was so little to do. They fed and watered Tuppence. They tended her wounds. Then there was nothing. She thought sitting in the box, writing and drawing, was a waste of time. She thought reading was a poor substitute for doing something.

Martin understood her impatience, yet resisted it. He knew she was right when she said, 'It's a poor holiday for you. You're not getting much out of it.'

She brought the skewbald for him to ride. They rode the moor, trying to rediscover the carefree enjoyment of a few months ago. They had picnics beside a stream. Jane rolled up her trouser-legs and taught him to tickle trout. She waded up the stream, her hands quietly exploring the darkness beneath the overhanging banks.

He tried to share her enthusiasms, but at the back of his mind he worried about Tuppence.

Even gymkhanas were disappointing because he was not riding the right pony. The skewbald did its best, but it was not fast enough or bold enough. It seemed to know that he did not really care.

Jane cared. She rode to win all the time. The chestnut knew what was expected of it and learned quickly. It liked jumping more than the helter-skelter games. It won its 13.2-and-under class at two gymkhanas.

Jane was triumphant. She had forgotten what would happen.

To Harvey gymkhanas were not holiday fun. They were shop-windows for his best ponies. A doctor offered sixty guineas for the chestnut, wanting a second pony for his daughter. Harvey refused it, knowing that a retired Army officer was watching the chestnut, comparing its performances at successive gymkhanas. Harvey guessed the officer would make an offer and that officer and doctor could become rivals, thus pushing up the price.

The chestnut won again. Jane rode it beautifully. Spectators around the ring applauded generously, recognizing her skill. Martin didn't applaud. He had seen Harvey talking with the doctor. He guessed what was about to happen.

The doctor offered eighty-five guineas and Harvey took it. One minute Jane was triumphant on the winner. The next she had nothing to ride. The chestnut was being driven away to the doctor's stable.

Martin saw her dismay. She had known it would happen, yet it still hurt. He saw the look of jealous hatred which she flashed to the doctor's daughter.

'My pony now,' the doctor's daughter said, rubbing it in. For the first time Martin saw that Jane was near tears.

She lost interest in the remaining gymkhanas of the season. She pretended that she didn't want to ride the skewbald because it was neither good enough nor keen enough. It would never win. But Martin guessed she stayed away because she didn't want to see the doctor's daughter on the chestnut.

They never mentioned the chestnut, pretending it had never been. But both read newspaper reports of gymkhanas. The chestnut was never among the winners. Perhaps it was not as clever a jumper as Jane had made it appear. But Martin thought it was unhappy. It hated gymkhanas without Jane.

This sense of mourning brought Jane and Martin close again. They spent the rest of the holiday at Shepherds Hill. They climbed trees. They found the cat's new kittens in the loft. They caught small trout with their hands. They were never far from Tuppence.

In September the holiday ended. Jane went back to her primary school and a term of revision before the eleven-plus. Martin went back to Miss Powell and geography in the Middle Ages.

He was twelve years old on October 10th. His mother wanted him to have a big party, inviting his school-friends, as many as he liked. The kitchen was big enough. The kitchen table had been long enough for big parties in the old days.

Martin wasn't sure. Twelve years old might be too old for parties. It was almost old enough to be a teenager.

'Rubbish,' his mother said. 'I always liked the parties you used to have. Invite as many as you like. We can use the Land Rover as well as the car for giving lifts.'

Martin invited seven from the school, including Miss Powell. Jane didn't need a formal invitation. She came over on the skewbald. She was carrying a case.

Martin wondered what was in it but his mother guessed. She showed Jane to a bedroom, helping her change from sweater and jodhpurs to a party dress. The transformation was startling. Martin hardly recognized her.

She helped his mother prepare the table while he showed his school-friends around the farm. They were delighted by the calves and young pigs. They kept pointing to the moor, astonished by its size, by the sense of space. Martin realized that most of them lived on housing estates or in terraces; small rooms and small gardens; conscious always of the people next door. He realized they were envying him so much space, so many animals. He wondered what they would have said had they come last winter.

He showed them Tuppence in the orchard. Six months ago she would have been excited by so many strangers. She would have pretended deep suspicion, as though each might have a bomb hidden somewhere. Then she would have shown off a little, rejecting their offers of friendship, playing hard-to-get. Not until they'd had enough of that would she have put aside all fears and come to see what their hands were offering.

Now she only stared, not interested in what their hands were offering. Now she looked dull and stupid. Now Martin had to call her, persuading her to be polite to his guests. It was a mistake.

When she came near the gate the school-friends saw the wrong side of her head. They didn't understand that it was better now, much better than it had been in May. They were shocked. They made expressions of disgust. They didn't want to touch her.

Martin saw their horror and guessed that Tuppence had seen it, too. Suddenly he hated them. He wanted them to go away, to stop insulting his brave little pony.

Only Miss Powell understood. She patted Tuppence, showing them that even a badly injured pony would respond to praise. But the visit to the orchard was a failure. The school-friends turned away, more interested in the pigs, the sheep, the hover of a hawk. Martin followed them to the house, to the table ready for tea.

His mother had spent days preparing. Nathan's wife had helped. There were jellies, meringues, cheese straws, iced cakes, sausage rolls, brandy snaps, trifles, biscuits. There were glass jugs of lemonade. In the centre was the official cake, fat with icing and decorated by twelve candles.

There was admiration for the cake, but the school-friends most admired the bowl of clotted cream. Its skin was a harvest colour. It was crinkled like the soles of your feet when you've been paddling. It looked too good to break with a spoon.

Martin realized that many of his friends had

never seen farmhouse cream. They thought cream was something in tins, bought by tourists and sent by post to Birmingham and Manchester. They had never eaten home-made bread and cream, with strawberry jam on top.

Mrs. Manningham offered them more and more, delighted by their appetites. They had polite slices of cake. They ignored the jellies and trifles. They kept asking for more cream, more jam. Only Jane didn't touch it. Clotted cream was no novelty to her. She preferred cheese straws and brandy snaps.

After tea they moved to the parlour. Mrs. Manningham tried to organize games, with prizes for everyone, but the interest was only polite. They did not become excited until Jane suggested the home-made band. Then some wanted the guitar, others the drums and cymbals. Martin raided the kitchen shelves for more saucepan-lids and tin plates. The more din, the higher their excitement.

He was surprised they could could find so much enjoyment so simply. Then he realized that this was the sort of din which could not be made in a terrace house or city flat. Too many neighbours; the baby in the next flat. There were always good reasons in a town or city for having to be quiet.

But there were no neighbours at Shepherds Hill. Only Nathan's wife lived near enough to hear, and she didn't mind. She was part of the party.

Martin thought that when it was all over, they would remember first the luxury of din, then the clotted cream, then the loneliness of the moor.

The party ended at eight. Miss Powell gave lifts to some. Mr. Manningham took others in the car.

Jane was the last to go. She stayed to help Nathan's wife tidy the parlour.

Then she changed from Jane-in-her-party-dress to Jane in sweater and jodhpurs. She saddled the skewbald and rode away. Not until he was watching her cross the bridge, only her yellow sweater showing in the fading light, did Martin realize something.

Other guests had given him the usual gifts; fountain pen, autograph book, construction kit, book tokens. Miss Powell had given a sketching pad and coloured pencils. Only Jane had not brought a gift.

He didn't care. Jane was a special friend, and special friends were more important than gifts. But there must be a reason. Perhaps Harvey had refused to give her money, refused to let her buy a gift. Perhaps Harvey had said, 'That boy's already got enough.' Martin could imagine him saying it.

It was true, too. He needed Jane more than he needed another construction kit, another pen or book.

He didn't find out what Jane was planning until the Autumn 'drift'.

This was the time of year when farmers drove mares and foals, colts and fillies off the moor for the big sale.

At one time all the community had taken part. Riders had been summoned by hunting horn, blown from the top of a tor, with the horn held against the granite to resound across the valley.

In those days there had been no fun which the

people had not made themselves. Moorland families of all ages had welcomed the chance to meet and ride and sip whisky, then to come home to a big supper of boiled ham and pork and quart mugs of ale. The ponies had been less important than the get-together.

Now there was television. Dartmoor families could watch all-in wrestling at Halifax or Rugby League at Wigan. They were no longer isolated, dependent on local events. So old customs had gone down and down until the 'drift' had become a small affair; a private arrangement among three or four neighbours with no big feast at the end.

There had been other changes.

The original Dartmoor breed had been crossed with New Forest and Shetland ponies to produce a small, tough mongrel which could work underground in the mines of Wales and the north. Hundreds each year had been sold to the pits. But the introduction of more and more machines had meant that the ponies had been needed less and less. For a time it had seemed that the breeding of wild ponies would cease to be profitable. Pessimists had pointed to more and more cars and vans on the roads. Nobody wanted little ponies, even those which could work hard on little food.

Then a new market had developed.

Children wanted ponies. They had bicycles. Their parents had cars for long journeys. But bicycles and cars were machines, and machines were not enough. Children begged and parents yielded. Those who couldn't afford to keep their own ponies paid the fees of riding stables.

Soon there were more riding stables, more young riders at hunts and gymkhanas. Pony clubs thrived. Small, tough ponies were in demand again.

But that was not the only market.

People in towns and cities kept more and more pets; and more and more pets, especially dogs and cats, meant big increases in the sale of tinned food for pets. This increased the demand for pony meat. Many of the older, less attractive ponies were sold to dealers and trucked away for slaughter.

The R.S.P.C.A. watched over the big sales. There had been much improvement in the feeding and watering of animals doomed to make long journeys. But many people were still concerned. Every year there were criticisms that Dartmoor farmers should show more interest; that their responsibilities did not end with the sale to dealers.

Jane's father was the leading pony-farmer in the neighbourhood. Other farms produced milk and beef and pork. They had only a few mares on the moor. Some had none. They preferred to turn out sheep. Harvey had only a few beef calves, only two sows. His main herd was the ponies. For him the 'drift' was the big day. If he had a good sale, with prices high, he was jubilant. If prices were low he had to struggle the rest of the year.

Two other farmers in the neighbourhood joined him in the 'drift'. Martin and Jane helped, too. She rode a new pony, bought cheaply because her father thought it would make a jumper. Martin rode the skewbald.

The day began quietly. They picked up the first mares about five miles away and drove them out of the valley to the high hill. Jane rode on one flank, Martin on the other. Harvey and his friends were bringing up the rear.

The wind was raw. Arrows of rain were sharp. The wild ponies wanted to stop and graze. They didn't want to be driven. But they were not frightened yet. They hadn't realized what the day meant.

Their fright quickened as the 'drift' picked up more and more. The bigger the moving herd, the bigger the fright. They knew now that this was no ordinary day. Some tried to break sideways. Then Martin or Jane headed them off. But their most persistent instinct was to go forward, faster and faster, their heads up and their fear trembling in the ground.

Mares hugged in their foals and the foals were bewildered. They were like refugee children who run with their parents without knowing why their parents are running.

Martin saw that some old mares were lame. They hobbled, their heads down. The lameness showed most when they trotted. But the yearling colts and fillies were bold, resisting this first hint that life was not all freedom and wild grass.

The men guessed the value of the year's crop as they ran. Not as many foals as in other years. That was a result of the long winter. But better than some had predicted.

Harvey counted his black-and-white yearlings and two-year-olds. They would fetch the best prices. 'Coloured' ponies were always popular with children and riding stables. That's why he kept a piebald stallion. It wasn't a good specimen, but its colour was important. Almost all its foals had the white markings which children liked.

Martin's pity went out to the hobbling mares. Dealers would buy them cheaply, but even low prices would satisfy Harvey. They had lived all their years on the moor, grazing where they could. Each year they had had foals which had finally been sold. They had cost him nothing, so Harvey could afford to sell them in their old age for whatever they would fetch. Even five pounds would be all profit.

Martin was sad for the head-down mares, but if he protested, he knew what Harvey would say.

'I sell ponies like your father sells bullocks.' That was how Harvey would begin. Then he would say that in his opinion ponies were cattle. That's how they had been described in the old days.

He kept them as cheaply as possible because that was good business. He sold them to the highest bidder because that also was good business. He couldn't understand the popular sympathy for ponies; the belief that ponies were superior to bullocks.

Martin knew it would be useless to argue. He watched the ragged army run down the long hill. They were very frightened now. They were running like the doomed. Harvey opened the gate to the walled field and in the ponies went, the old mares first, keeping their foals close, then the wilder colts and fillies.

A colt turned away from the gate, making a last bid for freedom. Jane headed it off. Harvey and the other men helped her chivvy it back to join the others.

Martin watched the old mares. They were tired their heads were low. But they were still sheltering their foals; standing between them and the men at the gate. They did not look up when the colts and fillies pounded around, looking for a way out. The old mares knew there was no way out.

Martin saw Harvey discussing with his friend what he would do. Yearling colts would be cut and turned back to the moor to grow another year Some fillies would be turned back, also, to become brood mares and ensure the supply next year Most of the others would be sold. Only the best would be kept in this field for Jane to break and school.

Harvey boasted of her skill to other farmers. H was proud of her refusal to let a pony win. Sh could be thrown three times in as many minutes but each time she would get back, riding out th bucking. Then she schooled them to traffic and ele mentary dressage; teaching them to respond to th touch of rein or knee or heel. Within six month each would be worth fifty pounds or more. Eight perhaps, if they proved as good as the chestnut and won prizes.

Harvey left the schooling, the riding to Jane. No until she had made the ponies as good as possible did he show new interest. Then he adverstised them in local newspapers, selling to parents in town and country who wanted reliable ponies for their chil dren. Sometimes he sold them readily. Sometime one or two were failures.

Tuppence had been one of them. Martin realized that if she had proved as clever as the chestnut, she would not have come to him. She would have been sold to somebody else long before his father had decided to buy.

Harvey came into the field, pointing with his whip, telling Jane what ponies would be kept for schooling. Martin watched the ponies milling round, telling himself that once Tuppence had been in the middle. He imagined how she had run, bewildered by the shouting, the arm-waving, the cracking of whips. He understood why she had been so nervous when she had come to Shepherds Hill.

He looked away. Near the field were the iron bars of the 'chute', down which the new stock would run for branding. He saw the branding-iron, with Harvey's emblem on the end. It was appied hot to the pony's rump. Stockholm tar was daubed on the wound, and for evermore the pony would have Harvey's mark.

Martin rebelled against the branding-iron. He knew there must be some proof of ownership. But he wished some other method could be found. There was some consolation in what Nathan had once said. Branding looked worse than it was. In a surprisingly short time the wound healed. Still Martin was not convinced. He imagined Tuppence as the branding-iron had come down. His throat tightened with sickness.

He saw Harvey choosing the young colts for cutting. This was another operation which had to be done, but which made him cringe. The cutting made geldings of colts. It changed their personalities, making them quiet, easy to handle, much easier to work. It also reduced fighting.

The best age for cutting was a year old, although some colts were cut as foals. It was as necessary to make geldings of colts as it was to make bullocks of bulls. But still Martin cringed. He didn't trust Harvey.

He saw Jane talking with her father. They were arguing. Then she pointed and Martin realized they were arguing about him. Her face was flushed, her eyes were angry. Martin knew that in this mood, Jane wouldn't give in easily.

He didn't want to be drawn into any row. He wanted to go home; to forget what would happen to these ponies, what might happen to the old mares before they were slaughtered. He was turning away as Jane reached him.

She held his arm, detaining him, beckoning her father. Harvey came slowly, reluctantly. Martin knew that in the argument Jane had won.

'Your birthday present,' she said. 'I didn't want to give you something, anything, like all the others.'

Martin saw her earnestness. He struggled to understand.

'I wanted to give you something special. Something you need now that Tuppence is no good.'

He understood. He was amazed. He wanted to say, 'Tuppence isn't finished.'

'She is,' Jane said. 'You'll never ride her again, you couldn't put a bridle on her. She'll never be good for anything except mooching round the orchard.'

Martin was frightened by her certainty. It sounded true. It sounded cruel.

'So you can have that colt – look.' She pointed to a black colt with white legs. 'My father agrees. For your birthday.'

Martin was bewildered by her generosity. He guessed she had been arguing for weeks; that her father had put her off with vague promises, not agreeing until their final argument in the field.

'You've had bad luck with Tuppence,' Jane said. 'Terribly bad luck. So here's another. You can break him yourself. Have some fun breaking him. You haven't had any fun out of Tuppence since what happened in May.'

Martin didn't understand all of it, but he guessed she was trying to make amends for what the Harvey herd had done to Tuppence. He was grateful. He was tempted. He looked at the black colt a long time, comparing its young strength with his cripple in the orchard.

He shook his head. He couldn't explain. He only knew that if he brought another pony to Shepherds Hill, Tuppence would be crestfallen, jealous.

'What do you mean – no?' Jane was incredulous. 'The orchard's big enough for two. You've got the stable for the winter. Tuppence can stay out.'

She had been planning it a long time. He saw her disappointment.

He knew she wouldn't understand. He didn't want to ride. That was not enough. He wanted the something which he shared with Tuppence. He saw

157

her disappointment turn to anger. He saw Harvey's relief. He tried to say, 'It's very generous – I appreciate . . .' But Jane flounced away. He guessed she was near tears.

Sadly he turned for home, walking across the heather, jumping the random streams. He had offended Jane. She wouldn't forgive easily. Now his only friend was Tuppence.

For weeks Jane didn't come to Shepherds Hill. His parents were disappointed. They supposed there had been a quarrel.

Once Mrs. Manningham risked a point-blank question. 'Why doesn't Jane come now?' But Martin didn't tell her about the black pony with the white legs. He was afraid his parents wouldn't understand.

He had begun to regret his refusal, partly because of Jane, partly because Tuppence was a poor companion.

Her head had healed. The vet seemed pleased. Only Martin realized how her temperament had changed.

No longer a comedienne, no longer a bold heroine, she wasn't recognizable as the pony who had swanked about. She looked much older. She scrounged moodily. Then she bit him.

He was in the orchard, sitting saddle-fashion on the low branch of a tree. She came behind, nudging for carrots. He showed her that he had no more. Then her teeth got his shoulder.

He thought it was a joke and waited for her to let go. She shook his shoulder. The shape of her head was thin and mean and evil. He shouted, threatening her with his fist for the first time. She flinched back. He put up a hand to his shoulder, astonished by the pain. He pulled long faces, trying to make her ashamed, and she mooched away, looking ashamed.

His mother saw the bruising when he was in the bath. She pointed and he keened his head around to admire the blue and red patches.

'Who did that?'

He answered, 'Tuppence,' knowing she would be surprised. He was laughing, making a joke of it.

But his mother didn't think it funny. She told his father and there was a moment of incredulity. Then they looked at each other, thinking the same thought.

'You can't be sure,' Mr. Manningham said. 'Not just one bite.'

His wife was sure. 'After all that boy's done. You'd think the animal would be grateful.'

Mr. Manningham shook his head with a rueful smile. He knew animals better than that.

He said, 'She wouldn't hurt him. Not unless . . .'

He stopped, not wanting to put it into words. His wife did it for him.

She said, 'Those injuries. They've affected her brain. That's the explanation.'

They shared a long look, realizing that a brain injury would make Tuppence dangerous. Too dangerous for a boy to handle.

# CHAPTER ELEVEN

MARTIN concealed most of the bites from his parents. Each was a bruise, the colour of a plum. They ached like tooth-ache.

A part of each ache was dismay that Tuppence could do it to him. He had imagined she would never harm him. Yet now her moods were sly. She pretended to be nudging for food, then suddenly nipped, her ears flat, her head ugly. On these occasions she looked a stranger.

He couldn't believe this was the pony of moorland rides, of the sledge and snow, of that cold hunt which had ended almost in disaster. He couldn't believe this was the tragic cripple who had crept to a stream. It seemed incredible that not so long ago he had sat in her box, sketching her and writing about her.

They had been deep friends then. Now she was sly and vicious. He dared not turn his back.

She got him one afternoon in late December. He had brought hay to the orchard because the winter grass was thin. She came behind him, apparently interested only in the hay. He stooped to put it down and as he turned away, she got his arm. Her strong teeth crushed in, her eyes stared. He opened his mouth in pain.

She let him go and he covered the arm, wrapping the pain against himself as though to warm it and comfort it. He shouted, calling her a pig.

Then he saw someone in the lane. He recognized the yellow sweater and for a moment, surprise took away the pain. It was two months since Jane had come to Shepherds Hill.

He knew she had seen. She climbed into the orchard and came towards the pony. She didn't ask about his arm. She seemed more interested in what was wrong with Tuppence.

After a while she said, 'You know what's wrong?'

Martin shook his head, ready to deny it if Jane said her brain was damaged.

'It's not her fault, it's what happens sometimes.'

Still Martin didn't understand.

Jane laughed as she said, 'Your little filly, she's a mare now. She's going to have a foal.'

Martin couldn't believe it. Then they both laughed, remembering that the day was Christmas Eve. The news was a kind of Christmas present.

They ran to the house to tell his parents. His father and Nathan came to the orchard to make sure. They nodded, sharing the laughter, the excitement. It ensured that this Christmas would be a great success.

Martin was usually disappointed by Christmas. It was never all that it promised. The best period was always the preparation. But this Christmas was exalted because the bad-tempered little mare was suddenly a heroine again. Martin wanted to mollycoddle her, but Nathan shook his head.

'She's all right. She likes to be out of doors. Just give her hay every day, but never try to shut her in.'

Jane rode over on Christmas morning. Gifts were exchanged. Mrs. Manningham welcomed her with ginger-wine and mince-pies. Nathan came into the kitchen for the traditional glass of whisky. It was a smiling day.

There was goose for Christmas dinner. Goose had been the traditional Christmas bird long before the turkey. In the old days the feathers and down had made pillows and eiderdowns for winter beds.

Every Dartmoor family had its special Christmas customs. Often it was the only meal of the year which all members of the family shared. Some made long journeys to preserve the custom. Places were kept for sons who were soldiers and sailors. Every mother hoped that by some magic those sons would arrive as other members of the family were sitting down to Christmas dinner.

At Shepherds Hill the custom was that Nathan and his wife should come to the farmer's table; sharing the goose, the pudding, the cream, the crackers and cigars. But Mrs. Manningham hesitated about inviting Jane to stay. She wasn't being unkind. She had been brought up to believe that Christmas dinner was a family affair. She thought Jane's parents would want her at home. But a 'phone call put that right.

No, Mrs. Harvey didn't mind. They never made

much of Christmas. It was a waste of time and money, making such a fuss.

So Jane stayed, pulling a cracker with Nathan, another with Mr. Manningham. Martin watched her enjoyment, wondering what Christmas was like in her home if she could be so excited by what he took for granted.

He liked having Nathan and his wife at the Christmas table. The day would have lacked something if they had remained in their cottage and eaten alone. It was never a quiet meal. It was never hurried. First the eating; that had to be serious to show Mrs. Manningham that she was appreciated. Then the talking. That was always merry.

Martin watched their faces, guessing that they were talking of the old days, of the men who were now faded names in the church-yard. He remembered those stories. They were like the stars; old yet always seeming to be new. His father's favourite story was about Great-Grannie Manningham who had driven a single-furrow plough, her skirt tucked up and her big boots striding. When there had been no horse for the plough, Great-Grannie had driven a cow.

This story always reminded Nathan of how bullocks had been used for all kinds of farm-work. They had been shod with half-shoes because of their cloven hooves. That had been before his time, but he had heard his father tell of it. Now and again the modern plough still turned up the crescents of iron which the bullocks had worn.

Martin could not follow the laughing talk, but one word was enough to enable him to share.

His own favourite story was of Great-Uncle Joseph, never called 'Joe' because the abbreviation would have done less than justice to his beard. Great-Uncle Joseph had driven a team of six horses, hauling timber. They had been great and strong, as proud as princes. They had got long tree-trunks around narrow corners, backing intelligently, then going forward and backing again, gaining inches each time. The story said that Great-Uncle Joseph had driven them by word of command only. No whip, no dragging at their mouths. 'Left' he had shouted, and the word had been enough.

Martin saw Jane's fascination. All the stories were new to her.

Mrs. Manningham and Nathan's wife rose quietly to clear away the plates. But the men did not move. They leaned back, smoking cigars. It was part of the custom that Nathan brought two cigars from his top pocket, offering one to the farmer. Then Mr. Manningham struck a match for Nathan and they puffed, making a Christmas smell.

For a while the talk died as they enjoyed their cigars. Then it began again. The farmer told about Holler Harry who had sung tenor at concerts. Nathan recalled Apple Annie who had told fortunes in tea-cups.

Martin saw Jane laughing and guessed they had come to the bit where Holler Harry swallowed his top set. He joined the laughter. His father saw him laughing and winked.

Mrs. Manningham and Nathan's wife came back to the table. They sat a long time, drinking tea, the women nibbling biscuits while the men puffed. Soon they would be going back to the yard and afternoon milking. But for this hour they had time for the stories they had not told since last year.

In the evening there was another custom. They played cards; Mr. Manningham and Nathan, Jane and Martin. The women sat by the fire, sewing and knitting because their fingers were never idle. The traditional game was half-penny nap. Martin won three-halfpence. Jane won sevenpence. Mr. Manningham lost and pretended to be broke.

Martin pecked glances at the clock, knowing it must be over soon. There were special concessions because it was Christmas, but even Christmas Day couldn't last for ever. Soon his mother would get up, saying, 'There's another day tomorrow,' as she always did. Soon Jane would leave and the big day would be over.

He tried to postpone the end by distracting them with questions. When would Tuppence have her foal? Was the piebald stallion the father?

'You got to wait,' Nathan said. 'It won't be until April. It takes eleven months to make a foal.'

Martin asked more questions, but they knew what he was doing and pointed to the clock.

His mother brought Jane's coat, signalling the end. But his father would not let Jane ride across the dark moor. She could leave the skewbald in the box. He would drive her home. Martin went with them. It was another way of prolonging the day. The journey was silent, for Jane was more tired than she would admit. On the way back

Martin fell asleep, leaning into his father's shoulder.

He didn't feel his father put an arm around him; didn't realize that his father drove slowly, making the evening last. He was dreaming of Tuppence and the foal.

In March Tuppence's moods became even more erratic. One minute she was all lean and nudge, as in the old days. The next she was snapping as though she hated him.

'It's what happens,' Nathan said. 'She turns on the one she likes best. It looks like hatred but it isn't. It's just her first foal and the weight hurts and it's all new to her.'

Martin knew that when the foal was born, Tuppence would be the only parent. There would be no father to share the responsibilities. He thought it a pretty poor arrangement; not as satisfactory as the birds, which shared the sitting and the feeding; not as noble as swans, which stayed together all their lives. The cob swan, like the dog fox, was a loyal father. Yet the piebald stallion would show no interest.

His poor little mare was alone, with none to protect her in the night or to brandish away the flies during the day. Perhaps that explained her moodiness.

'Better bring her in,' Mr. Manningham said. 'Her time's near.'

Jane helped prepare the box. They made the straw specially deep, like a hospital bed. They wanted to do all they could, feeling helpless because they could do so little.

Tuppence did not want to come. She had to be coaxed out of the orchard and down the lane. She sniffed the straw suspiciously. She pawed it up. Whenever the door opened, she looked yearningly to daylight.

'It's cold out there,' Martin said. 'It's going to rain. You're better in here where it's warm.'

His father thought she would soon settle down, but Tuppence did not. She pawed the door, telling them plainly. When they did not heed, she turned and let out her back legs making the door tremble.

'What's the matter?' Martin asked. 'She'll damage herself.'

Nathan explained that she wanted to get out to the orchard because that was near her natural home on the moor. She didn't want to be pampered. She wanted the grass and the stars. She wanted to have her foal as she herself had been born. Without fuss, in some secret corner, with none to know until it was all over.

'She's a tough breed,' Nathan said. 'That's the way foals are born in a tough breed. They don't like fussing. Most of all they don't like being watched.'

Sadly Martin let her have her way. He took her back to the orchard. She went at once to a corner where the grass was coarse and the nettles were thick. She walked around and around, trampling down the grass and nettles, making it a secret place, as round and private as a nest.

It was the same instinct which compelled birds to build in a secret place; which made a dog turn round and round before it settled. She preferred

167

this place which she had made herself to the deep straw. She wanted it to be secret.

'Stay away,' Nathan said. 'Don't go near.'

Martin wanted to argue. Staying away seemed cruel, as though he didn't care.

'Never interfere,' Nathan said. 'You know what the vet said – never interfere with nature till something goes wrong. Then – if nature can't do it – that's the time to help.'

Martin thought about it. It seemed indifferent, the sort of thing which Harvey would say because he couldn't be bothered. Yet it made sense when you realized that every year foals were born in the secret places of the moor.

'She's young,' Nathan said. 'She's tough. The worst thing you can do is interfere.'

Martin watched her stand near the patch she had made. She was looking towards them, defending her corner. Her expression was defiant.

He asked, 'When will it be?'

Nathan put up two fingers, then three. Then he shrugged, showing that he did not really know. He could only guess. Two days. Three perhaps.

Martin thought it would be sooner, perhaps tonight. He didn't know how he knew. Perhaps the way she stood, defending her corner, perhaps that was a sign.

The more he thought about it, the more he was sure. In the darkness of nine o'clock, before he went to bed, he came to the orchard and peered through the trees. There was a dark shape in the corner. That must be her.

He wanted to call, to climb the gate and go to

her, but Nathan's warning was in his head. He knew that something terrible and wonderful was about to happen, and that this time Tuppence must be alone.

'I told him two or three days,' Nathan said. 'So he wouldn't worry like.'

Mr. Manningham nodded. That was good sense.

'But it could be tonight,' Nathan said. 'I wouldn't be surprised.'

They looked up to the ceiling, listening to Mrs. Manningham talking to the boy. He wasn't asleep and there was school tomorrow.

'So I thought,' Nathan said, 'I'd keep an eye on her, just in case.'

Mr. Manningham answered, 'That could mean going all night.'

Nathan shrugged. It had happened before with ewes and heifers. He would rather go without sleep than risk an accident; a dead foal in the morning.

'It might be all right,' he said. 'In that case she won't need anyone. But you never know. It's her first and somebody ought to be listening, just in case.'

Mr. Manningham reached for his coat. 'I'll come with you. If anything happened to that little mare ...'

His wife came down as they were preparing to go out. She said, 'He's worrying. He thinks it might be tonight.'

Mr. Manningham was surprised. 'Nathan told him – two or three days.'

'You can't deceive him. He knows.'

'How, then?'

Mrs. Manningham didn't know. She said, 'Anything about that pony, he seems to know.'

The father found his torch. 'Whatever you do, don't tell him. It might not be tonight, and if it is, anything might happen.'

He and Nathan went out to the darkness. Their boots knew every stone in the lane. They did not show a torch because any light would frighten the mare.

They came quietly to the gate and listened. They heard her breathing. The sound was hurt and laboured. Nathan glanced to the farmer. It was going to be tonight.

They saw something pale, fluttering like a balloon. It was the first water-bag.

They waited for the pause. There was always a pause at this stage. It was nature's way of giving the mare time to recover from the first great pains. They couldn't hear her breathing. There was the quiet of rest.

Then the pains began again. Her breathing became loud and strained. The farmer felt the wetness of his hands. He had seen it a thousand times with cows and sheep and pigs. But he hadn't become hardened to it. It sounded torturous. You could believe in these minutes that nature was cruel, demanding the impossible.

The sounds went on so long that Nathan put a foot on the gate, ready to go to her, sure that the foal's shoulders and withers had become wedged.

The farmer stopped him with a touch. They

listened again. The mare was still making her struggling sounds. Then came the last, a supreme effort.

'Good,' Mr. Manningham said.

It meant the foal was born. Both climbed the gate, moving cautiously through the darkness.

She was too exhausted to hear them. She had dropped to the grass. She was lying like the dying. Her neck was stretched, her eyes were staring. She was breathing deeply, her side heaving as though her heart had burst.

Nathan stooped to the foal. It was gasping. Then the sound changed and it was breathing. Its breaths were weak but Nathan knew better than to touch. Within two minutes the breathing was steady.

He picked it up and carried it to the mare's head. She got up, heaving herself with a mighty effort. She dropped her nose to the foal, touching it but not licking.

'Her first foal,' Nathan said.

He was making excuses because she did not immediately dry and clean the foal. He took a bag from his pocket and plunged in a hand.

His hand came out with something white like frost. It was salt. He rubbed it into the coat of the foal and the mare tasted the salt, then licked. At first she was licking only because of the salt. Then nature took over and she licked until the foal was dry and clean.

Mr. Manningham and Nathan sat on their heels, waiting for the foal to stand. Within fifteen minutes it was trying. In half an hour it had succeeded, although it fell at once.

It struggled again, its long legs strengthening. Shakily it reached for the first milk. It couldn't find the teat, so Tuppence reached back with her nose and bumped, guiding it.

They knew it had found as soon as its tail began to throb. The urgency in its tail was comic. Nathan and the farmer exchanged a grin.

Mr. Manningham asked, 'What you think about the mare?'

Nathan considered her a long time, then nodded. She needed help. To help her now would not be interfering.

The farmer hurried to the kitchen. He found treacle and the whisky bottle. He measured a little whisky into treacle and water. He carried the bowl to her. She took it greedily.

'More again in an hour,' Mr. Manningham said. 'Then she'll be all right.'

Three hours later, when the foal was strong and the terrible sounds of birth seemed a long time ago, Nathan brought her bran mash and hay. He felt her ears, her nostrils, looking for signs of cold.

'She's all right,' Nathan said. 'Next time she'll find it easier.'

Mr. Manningham looked at the colt foal, smiling as he imagined Martin's excitement in the morning.

Martin shouted as though they didn't know. He waved to his parents to come. He ran to tell Nathan, and the old farm-hand said nothing of what had happened in the night.

He only warned, 'Don't fuss her, mind. It's the

first time she's been a mother and she takes it very serious. She don't want anyone to come between her and the foal.'

Martin went as near as he dared, then sat in a tree, watching and talking, telling Tuppence what a wonderful mare she was. He didn't want to leave when his mother called him to breakfast. He ate hurriedly then ran back, stealing more minutes before it was time for the drive to school.

The first person he told was Miss Powell. He made it the most wonderful foal in the world, and she understood and promised to come on Sunday.

'Although you mustn't go near,' Martin said. 'Tuppence is still jealous. I don't think she can believe it herself hardly.'

Miss Powell smiled, remembering the days, not long ago, when he had refused to speak. She listened to him telling other pupils. He had got over that now. He trusted others to understand what he was saying and to share his excitement. Now he was no longer a little boy on the outside, shut up in silence and wounded by the fact of sudden deafness. He had begun to realize that deafness was not the end.

Jane rode over in the evening. She sat with him in the tree, watching the foal, inventing improbable names for it. They were entranced by the magic of new life.

Within a month the little fellow would begin to eat grass. A month later he would take corn from your hand. Through the summer he would run with Tuppence, showing off his young exuberance;

running, then standing, then running again, going nowhere, making his mother seem slow and staid.

Tuppence would watch his antics with benign pride, sometimes glancing to Martin to see if he appreciated. This would be another part for her to play. The comedienne, the heroine, had become a proud mother. Sure that her offspring was rather remarkable. Sure also that this was not prejudice.

The foal and Tuppence would be inseparable until October. Then he would be weaned. The strong link between mother and son would be broken, never to be felt again. They might tolerate each other for a while, but there would be a widening gulf. Tuppence would complain that the young fellow was a nuisance, pestering her to play silly games, showing no respect at all for an older generation. Meanwhile the foal would think she was old and dull, content to stand and dream, a kill-joy who had never been young.

Soon the young fellow would be on his own. If he tried to play with Tuppence, she would kick him away. He would have nothing to do except chase his shadow and grow and strengthen until he was two years old. Then he would be ready to be saddled.

Martin looked ahead to that far-off day. I'll do it gently, he thought. I'll show him there's nothing to fear. That was the important thing; the thing which needed time and patience; the taking away of fear.

Nathan would help during the lunging, teaching

the beginner to go round and round in a circle. Jane would help during the schooling.

Their combined care would teach the new pony that hunting, jumping, racing was not hard work. It was fun. That was important, Martin thought. You had to impose discipline, because a wayward pony was dangerous. But you must also preserve the spirit.

He hoped the foal had inherited his mother's spirit. She was bold, he thought. She never knew when she was beaten. Perhaps she would always be old and slow to the foal. But he would always think of her as she had been that day when the chestnut had looked down its nose.

'She was my first,' he told the foal. 'She'll always be something special to me.'

Tuppence moved from her private corner. She came slowly to the tree, and the foal followed, staggering on legs not yet sure of themselves. Tuppence reached the tree and nudged and looked up.

It seemed she was apologizing for those moods of snapping. She wanted it to be as it used to be. He reached in a pocket for slices of mangold. She liked it for the juice. She took what he offered, then leaned against him, asking to be scratched. He rubbed his fingers up and down her neck, and the little mare hung her head and dreamed. Meanwhile the foal looked up, its face asking as many questions as a kitten.

Slowly Martin reached to touch, showing his hand so it would not be frightened. He touched the foal with one hand and scratched the mare with the other. He was not laughing, but there was laughter in his heart.

Martin did not feel resentful of what had happened to his ears. He did not feel different and shut in. He didn't suspect all the world of laughing at him.

He felt rich.